Leonard Grover

Dooner's Trip

Leonard Grover

Dooner's Trip

ISBN/EAN: 9783337144982

Printed in Europe, USA, Canada, Australia, Japan

Cover: Foto ©Andreas Hilbeck / pixelio.de

More available books at **www.hansebooks.com**

DOONER'S TRIP.

A Comedy in Four Acts.

TRANSLATED AND FREELY ADAPTED FROM THE FRENCH

BY

LEONARD GROVER,

Author of "Treasure Trove," "Our Boarding-House," "H. R. H.
the Prince," "My Son-in-Law," "Bad Dickey," etc.

Entered, according to Act of Congress, in the Office of the Congressional
Librarian, in the year 1880.

N. B.—Full description of the Scenes forwarded upon application.

———◆———

NEW YORK:
SAMUEL FRENCH & SON,
PUBLISHERS,
38 E. 14th St., Union Square.

LONDON:
SAMUEL FRENCH,
PUBLISHER,
89, STRAND.

CHARACTERS IN THE COMEDY.

• ————

CADWALADER DOONER—An opulent Pork-Packer. Age, 50.

COL. CALHOUN BAUMGARTNER—Ex-Colonel "Louisiana Tigers."
Age, 50.

GRATEFUL HUCKLESTONE—Clerk in a Sugar-Refinery. Age, 55.

HORACE WALBRIDGE—Partner in the Sugar-Refinery. One of
"Mrs. Timmerhouse's best society." Age, 28.

WILLIE RITTENHOUSE—Partner in the Banking House of Bombax, Traquire & Co. Also one of "Mrs. Timmerhouse's best
society." Age, 25.

JOSEPH—Faithful decayed "Tiger," attached to the Colonel.
Age, 60.

MRS. CAROLINE DOONER—Wife of the opulent P. P. Cadwalader's Caroline. Age, 45.

MISS JOSEPHINE DOONER—The pretty blonde daughter of the
Dooners. Age, 19.

MRS. LUCINDA SPOOPENDYKE—A widow with the Stock in a
valuable Silver Mine to place. *Looks* 35.

MISS CLARA SPOOPENDYKE—Her niece, willing to take the one
that is left. Age, 21.

> ALICE—Servant-maid of the Dooners.
>
> LANDLORD of the Museum Hotel.
>
> A GUIDE to under the Falls.
>
> AN INDIAN SALESWOMAN.
>
> PHOTOGRAPH TOUTER.
>
> TELEGRAPH BOY.
>
> R. R. CONDUCTOR.
>
> R. R. OFFICIAL.
>
> PORTER.
>
> Travellers, etc., etc., etc.

————

TIME—The Present, Midsummer.

COSTUMES—Appropriate, Travelling and Society.

SCENES—Philadelphia R. R. Depot. Niagara Falls, Canada side.
Dooner's Villa.

ACTION takes place within five weeks.

DOONER'S TRIP.

ACT I.

SCENE.—*Interior Penn. R. R. Depot, Philadelphia. Scene rakes the stage* R. & L., *making angle* U. C. *Entrances* R. & L. *First, large arch in* R. *discloses high paling fence, beyond which the rears of departing trains are visible. At each second gong a train moves off. Telegraph office in angle* U. S. *Large opening in* L. C. *leading to ladies' waiting-room discloses periodical-stand. Small square opening* D. S., *through which tickets are sold. Guard-railing in front of this. Purchasers of tickets form line facing* U. S., *and exit through arch.*

TELEGRAPH BOY. Telegraph to all parts of the world. Rate to New York, only fifteen cents.

HUCKLESTONE. L. 1 E. (*To himself.*) This Dooner doesn't come ; here's a good hour that I've been waiting for him.

TEL. BOY. Telegraph to all parts of the world. Rate to New York, only fifteen cents.

HUCK. It was definitely settled for him to start early this morning for Niagara Falls, with his wife and daughter. (*With sarcasm.*) These pork-packers who go to Niagara ! These pork-packers who have half a million dollars ! These pork-packers who keep a carriage ! What an epoch ! what a condition of things ! As for me, I earn barely $1500 a year working and fretting in a sugar-refinery office. We frequently have two customers a week ; but there I am kept whether they come or not, reading the newspapers for five hours a day. This morning I demanded leave of absence, I said I was sick. I got it. It is absolutely necessary I should see Dooner before he departs. I want to have him lend me three hundred dollars. He'll put on the benevolent, assume the important—give me advice—a pork-packer. That's what galls me. But why doesn't he come ? They said he took the early express. (*To official who passes followed by a traveller.*) Mister, what time does the Niagara express leave ?

OFFICIAL. (*Brusquely.*) Ask the conductor.

HUCK. (*Aside.*) Thank you, Mister Hog. (*To* CONDUCTOR.) Mr. Conductor, what time does the Niagara express leave ?

CONDUCTOR. (*Brusquely.*) That's not my business. See the time-table. (*Pointing to it.*)

HUCK. Thank you. (*Aside.*) They are polite, these railroad men. If ever I catch one of them in the sugar refinery— Well, let's see the time-table. [*Exit through arch.*

[*Enter* DOONER, MISS DOONER, *and* JOSEPHINE, *following an official, from opening* L. C.]

DOON. This way. Don't leave us, we can never find ourselves. Where is our baggage ? (*Looking off.*) Ah ! all right. Who has got the umbarellas ?

JOSEPHINE. I have, papa.

DOON. And the lunch, and my dressing-case ?

MRS. D. Here they are.

DOON. And my Derby ? Oh ! it's left in the carriage. (*Starting and stopping.*) Ah, no ! I got it in my hand. Heavens ! but it's warm.

MRS. D. It's your fault. You hurried us—you urged us. I don't like to take a trip in this style.

DOON. It's the starting ! Once we are started, all will be easy. Stay here, I'm going to buy the tickets. (*Giving his hat to* JOSEPHINE.) Take care of my Derby. (*To an official.*) Three tickets for Niagara Falls.

OFF. (*Brusquely.*). It isn't opened yet ; in a quarter of an hour.

DOON. (*To* OFFICIAL.) I beg your pardon, it's the first time I've been to Niagara this way. (*Returning to his wife.*) We are ahead of time.

MRS. D. There ! When I told you we had plenty of time, you wouldn't let us eat our breakfast.

DOON. It's much better to be here early. We can look at the depot. (*To* JOSEPHINE.) Very well, my daughter, are you contented ? Here we are started. In a few moments more and rapid as the arrow from the bow—we throw ourselves through Mannyunk—on, on to Niagara. Have you brought the opera-glass ?

MRS. D. Yes, certainly.

JOS. Now I don't mean to reproach you, but for more than two years you have promised me this trip.

DOON. My child, it was necessary that I should watch the market—what fluctuations in mess, what capers in sides, what jumps in whole hogs. A merchant can't leave his exchange as easily as a young miss can her boarding-school. Then I waited that your school-days might terminate, in order to complete your education by causing to shine before your eyes the grandest spectacle in all nature.

MRS. D. Come, Dooner, are you going to continue in that style ?

Doon. What?

Mrs. D. Making speeches in a depot.

Doon. I don't make speeches. I school the imagination of our daughter. (*Taking a memorandum-book from pocket.*) See, my child, behold! a dairy. I mean a da-iry—no, a di-ary that I have bought for you.

Jos. What for, papa?

Doon. To write on one side our expenses, and on the other our impressions.

Jos. What impressions?

Doon. Our impressions of the trip. You write and I will dictate.

Mrs. D. How? You are going to make an author of yourself now?

Doon. It isn't a matter of making myself an author. I may have had literary aspirations in the past. The fluctuations in the pork market have subdued them. But it appears to me that a man of the world might have thoughts, ideas, impressions more or less brilliant, and might be able to recall them through a da-iry—no, a di-ary.

Mrs. D. That'll be huge.

Doon. (*Aside.*) That's the way she is every time that she doesn't get her tea the moment she's out of bed.

Employee. (*Enters from arch up.*) Mister, here are your trunks. Do you want to get them checked?

Doon. Certainly, certainly; but not before I've counted them. Because when you know how many— One -two—three—four —five—six—my wife, seven, my daughter, eight, and myself, nine. We are nine pieces.

Emp. Come ahead.

Doon. Let's hurry. (*Going.*)

Emp. Not that way—this way.

Doon. All right. (*To the ladies.*) Wait for me there. Don't stir, don't get lost.   [*Exit.*

Jos. Poor papa, what trouble he gives himself!

Mrs. D. He's like a hen on a hot griddle.

Hor. (*Enters. Porter follows with baggage.*) I don't know yet where 1 go. Wait! (*Seeing* Josephine.) It is she. I have not been mistaken. (*He salutes* Josephine, *who bows.*)

Mrs. D. (*To* Josephine.) Who is that gentleman?

Jos. It's a young man with whom I danced last week at Mrs. Timmerhouse's reception.

Mrs. D. Ah! Mrs. Timmerhouse's. (*Bows to* Horace.)

Hor. (*Bowing.*) Mrs. Dooner. Miss Josephine. What a happy coincidence! The ladies are about to leave?

Mrs. D. Yes, sir.

Hor. Going to New York, without doubt?

Mrs. D. No, sir.

Hor. To Long Branch, perhaps?

MRS. D. No, sir.

HOR. Pardon, madam, I thought if my services—·

EMP. Mister, you've just got time to get your baggage checked.

HOR. That's so. (*Aside.*) I thought I'd be able to find out where they were going before buying my ticket. (*Saluting.*) Mrs. Dooner. Miss Josephine. (*Aside.*) They leave, that's the principal thing. (*To* EMPLOYEE.) Come on. [*Exit through arch.*

[MRS. SPOOPENDYKE *and* CLARA *enter hastily part way, as though watching.*]

MRS. S. I told you, Clara. It's Mr. Walbridge.

CLA. Yes, Aunty. My! it's absurd.   [*Exit both.*

MRS. D. He's very good looking.

[*Enter* WILLIE, *followed by* COACHMAN.]

WILL. Carry my valise to the baggage-master. I will follow. (EMPLOYEE *exits.*) (*Perceiving* JOSEPHINE.) It is she. (*Bows.*)

MRS. D. Who is that gentleman?

JOS. It's another young man who danced with me at Mrs. Timmerhouse's reception.

MRS. D. Mrs. Timmerhouse's. (*Bows.*)

WILL. (*Bowing.*) Mrs. Dooner. Miss Josephine. What a happy coincidence. The ladies are going to leave?

MRS. D. Yes, sir.

WILL. The ladies are going to New York, without doubt?

MRS. D. No, sir.

WILL. To Long Branch, probably.

MRS. D. (*Aside.*) Just like the other. (*Aloud.*) No, sir.

WILL. Pardon, madam, I thought if my services—

MRS. D. (*Aside.*) Mrs. Timmerhouse's young men are all alike.

WILL. (*Aside.*) I haven't advanced very much. I will check my baggage and then return. (*Bowing.*) Mrs. Dooner. Miss Josephine.   [*Exit* L. 1 E.

[MRS. SPOOPENDYKE *and* CLARA *enter as before.*]

MRS. S. There, didn't I tell you, Clara, it's Mr. Rittenhouse?

CLA. Yes, Aunty. My! It's absurd.   [*Exit both.*

MRS. D. That's a very good-looking young man. But what on earth is your father doing? My feet ache standing here.

HUCK. (*Enters. Aside.*) I was mistaken, the train does not leave for an hour yet.

JOS. Hah! Mr. Hucklestone.

HUCK. (*Aside.*) Here they are at last.

MRS. D. How do you come to get away from the sugar-refinery?

HUCK. I demanded leave of absence. My dear madam, I didn't want to let you go away without saying good-by.

MRS. D. How? That's why you came. It's very kind.

HUCK. But I don't see Dooner.

JOS. Papa is busy with the baggage.

DOON. (*Enters arch.*) The tickets first. All right.

HUCK. Ah, here he is. Good morning, old friend.

DOON. (*Very busy.*) Ah, it's you! You are very kind to come to see me off. Pardon, I must get my tickets. (*He leaves 'im.*)

HUCK. He is polite.

DOON. (*To* OFFICIAL.) Mister Conductor, Mister Agent, Mister General Superintendent, they won't check my baggage before I have bought my tickets.

OFF. (*Arch up.*) It isn't open—wait.

DOON. Wait, and over there they told me to hurry. (*Coming front.*) I'm bothered.

MRS. D. And my feet ache standing here.

DOON. Very well, sit down. Don't you see there are benches. You are very good to stand there like two posts. Why don't you sit down?

MRS. D. You yourself told us not to stir. You are insupportable.

DOON. Now, Caroline.

MRS. D. Your trip! I've had enough of it already.

DOON. It's easy to see that you haven't had your tea. There, now, go sit down.

MRS. D. (*Sitting with* JOSEPHINE.) Very well, but hurry yourself.

HUCK. (*Aside.*) A nice little family.

DOON. (*To* HUCK.) She's always like that when she misses her tea in the morning. You good Hucklestone! It was very neat, your coming to see us off.

HUCK. Yes. I wanted to talk to you about a little business.

DOON. And my baggage resting there on a truck. I'm very uneasy. (*Aloud.*) You good, kind Hucklestone! It was very amiable for you to see us off. (*Aside.*) I must go there.

HUCK. I want to ask a little favor of you.

DOON. Of me?

HUCK. I'm a little pressed, and if you are willing to advance me three hundred dollars.

DOON. Now here?

HUCK. I believe I've always paid you the money that you have lent me.

DOON. It's no matter about that.

HUCK. I beg your pardon. I believe it should be considered. My month's salary of $125 is due in four weeks, and in two months after that I shall have $250 more due, and if you haven't confidence in me I will give you an order.

DOON. Nonsense, are you a fool?

HUCK. (*Dryly.*) Thank you.

DOON. Why do you come to me to ask this, just at the moment I am about leaving? I have drawn exactly the money necessary for my trip.

Huck. If that's your style, let me say no more about it. I will address a banker who demands a half per cent a month of me. I shan't die.

Doon. (*With pocketbook.*) See, don't feel so bad. There— there it is, $300. But don't speak about it before my wife.

Huck. (*Taking the money.*) I understand. She's so stingy.

Doon. How? stingy!

Huck. I mean to say that she has ideas of her own.

Doon. It's necessary to have, my friend, it's necessary.

Huck. (*Dryly.*) Well, that's $300 that I owe you. Good- by. (*Aside.*) What a bother about $300. And they go to Niagara. Pork-packers! Humph!   [*Exit* L. 1 E.

Doon. All right, he's gone. He didn't even say thank you! But at the bottom I believe he loves me. (*Seeing the ticket office open.*) Ah! jingo, they are selling the tickets. (*He throws him- self into the line.*)

Traveller. Pay attention, sir.

Emp. Take your turn, Mister, you there.

Doon. And my baggage, and my wife. (*Taking end of line.*)

[Colonel *and* Joseph *enter, the latter with a bag.*]

Col. You understand me?

Jo. Yes, my commander.

Col. And if she asks where I am, when I will return, you answer that you know nothing about it. I never want to hear speak of her again.

Jo. Yes, my commander.

Col. You say to Ida that all is at an end. Completely fin- ished.

Jo. Yes, my commander.

Doon. I've got my tickets now for the baggage.   [*Exit.*

Col. You understand me thoroughly?

Jo. Begging your pardon, my commander, it's no use your going.

Col. Why?

Jo. Because, when he returns, my commander will resume with Miss'Ida.

Col. Oh!

Jo Then it's money in your pocket, not to quit her. These little differences always cost something to my commander.

Col. Ah! this time it's serious. Ida has spurned my affec- tion and the kindness I have shown her.

Jo. They say that she ruins you, my commander. There was another nigger minstrel came this morning; and the nigger minstrels are like the army-worms when they commence to come.

Col. On my return I will arrange all my affairs. Good-by.

Jo. Good-by, my commander.

COL. (*Going and returning.*) You will write me at Clifton, Canada. You will tell me all the news about your health.

JO. (*Flattered.*) My commander is very kind.

COL. And afterward you will tell me if any one feels chagrined at my departure ; if any one cries—weeps—sheds tears ?

JO. Who, who, my commander ?

COL. By heavens ! she, Ida.

JO. You will take her back, my commander ?

COL. Never.

JO. This makes the eighth time. It gives me pain to see a brave man like you harassed by creditors and for whom—for a—

COL. Never mind, all right, give me my valise and write me at Clifton, to-morrow, or this evening. Good-by.

[Exit arch up.

JO. Good luck, my commander. (*Aside.*) He'll be back before a week. Oh ! my commander. *[Exit 1 L.*

MRS. D. (*Coming forward.*) I'm tired of waiting.

DOON. (*Enters.*) Well, at last the thing is done. I've got my tickets and I've got my checks.

MRS. D. Thank patience !

PORTER. Sir, don't forget the Porter if you please.

DOON. O yes ; wait. (*He brings his wife and daughter near.*) What do you think I ought to give him ; ten cents ?

[Gong ready.

MRS. D. Fifteen.

JOS. A quarter.

DOON. Very well, a quarter goes. Take it, my boy.

PORTER. Thank you, sir.

DOON. One moment, Josephine. Take your d-a—di-ary and write.

MRS. D. Already !

DOON. Expenses : Carriage, a dollar fifty ; railroad, $33.75 ; porter, 25 cents.

JOS. It's done.

DOON. Wait—impressions.

MRS. D. He's positively insupportable.

DOON. Adieu, Philadelphia, City of Brotherly Love, where every man's heart and hand— (*Gong sounds. People hurry in.*)

MRS. D. There's the bell. You'll make us miss the train.

DOON. Come along, we will finish that later. (*They hurry in.*)

[HORACE *and* WILLIE *both run in and hit each other at opposite sides in front of ticket hole.*]

WILL. Take care there.

HOR. Pay attention yourself.

WILL. (*Astonished.*) Horace !

HOR. Why, Will !

WILL. You are leaving ?

HOR. This instant, and you ?

WILL. I also.

HOR. That's delightful. We'll take the trip together. I have got some excellent cigars. And where are you going?

WILL. My dear boy, I don't know yet.

HOR. Ha! that's odd. No more do I. I have taken a ticket as far as Elmira.

WILL. Indeed! and so have I. I am in pursuit of a charming young lady.

HOR. Hello! So am I.

WILL. The daughter of a pork-packer.

HOR. Dooner?

WILL. Dooner.

HOR. It's the same lady.

WILL. But I love her, my dear Horace.

HOR. I love her just as much, my dear Will.

WILL. I want to marry her.

HOR. I—I am going to ask her hand, which is about the same thing.

WILL. But we can't both marry her.

HOR. It's forbidden in Philadelphia.

WILL. What shall we do? .

HOR. It's very simple. Since we are on the same journey, let us gayly continue our trip—try to please, to make her love us, each one for himself.

WILL. (Smiling.) Then it's a tournament?

HOR. A loyal battle, and friendly. If you are the conqueror, I will bow my head. If I succeed, you yield gracefully to me. Is it a bargain?

WILL. Bravo! I accept.

HOR. The hand before the battle.

WILL. And the hand and heart after. *Shake hands.* (*Go for tickets.*)

[*Enter* MRS SPOOPENDYKE *and* CLARA.]

MRS. S. Now I hope you are satisfied, Clara.

CLARA. Yes, Aunty. My! it's absurd.

MRS. S. I had no sooner determined to follow this millionaire pork-packer to Niagara, for I learned where he was going, than I find Mr. Walbridge and Mr. Rittenhouse in pursuit.

CLARA. Yes, Aunty. My! it's quite absurd.

MRS. S. What are they after? I ask myself. They don't want to get him to take shares in a mine. I do. I want to monopolize the entire mining operations of the Dooners. What is their little game, Clara?

CLARA. Yes, Aunty.

MRS. S. I tumbled.

CLARA. What, Aunty?

MRS. S. I tumbled to their precious dodge.

CLARA. Perhaps.

MRS. S. Dooner is rich. Dooner has a daughter, an only daughter. They are both after Josephine.

CLARA. Why, it's absurd !

MRS. S. They are both eligible, rich, good-looking.

CLARA. Very.

MRS. S. One of them will get refused.

CLARA. I should hope so.

MRS. S. A man piqued with a refusal jumps at the next girl he sees.

CLARA. Yes.

MRS. S. And there is your chance, my dear.

CLARA. My, Aunty, it's absurd !

MRS. S. We follow. We cultivate the Dooners, and when the precious moment arrives you shall be Mrs. Walbridge or Mrs. Rittenhouse. And I—I shall dispose of some shares in the new mine.

DOON. (*Enters.*) I tell you that I've got time.

HOR. Hold ! Our father-in-law. [*Gong ready.*

DOON. (*To book-stall.*) Young woman, I want a book for my wife and my daughter, a book that doesn't talk about love, nor money, nor politics, nor marriage, nor death.

HOR. (*Aside.*) '' Robinson Crusoe.''

BOOKMAN. I've got it. Here you are, sir. (*Giving book.*)

DOON. (*Reading.*) The History of the Permanent Exposition Twenty-five cents. You swear to me that— (*Bell sounds, he runs.*) Good-day.

WILL. Follow him.

HOR. Follow, follow. I wish I knew where we are going.

MRS. S. Follow him. Follow them, Clara.

[*Passengers hurry in with satchels, etc.*

DOONER. (*Returning.*) Adieu, Philadelphia, City of Brotherly Love— (*Gong sounds.*)

TEL. BOY. Telegraphs to all parts of the world. Rate to New York only fifteen cents !

ACT II.

SCENE.—*Niagara Falls on the Canada side. The water on the Canada side rolls over the ledge which rakes from L. to C. U. S. The American fall pours over, facing R. C. The horizon discloses the village of Niagara in the distance. Hotels, etc. Tiny American flags, Goat Island, foliage, rocks, etc. A ground row of broken stone and shrubbery masks the fall, behind which rises the vapor from the falls, and against which is thrown a rainbow. The distant sky is of a deep transparent blue, which works with lights down for rain-storm. At right U. S. is a small shed with door practicable, labelled "Under the Falls."*
A two-story building with piazza, practicable door, exterior lamps (unlighted), sign "Museum Hotel," from R. proscenium to third entrance. A table and some chairs are in front of the hotel. An English flag from top of hotel.
A high ornamental garden wall skirts the left from proscenium to third entrance, behind which are trees and shrubbery.
☞ *THIS SCENE, conceded by excellent judges one of the most effective, WILL BE PATENTED. The cost of construction is extremely moderate. Invented in all details by Leonard Grover.*

[*Enter at rise around corner of hotel,* HORACE, WILLIE, MRS. SPOOPENDYKE, CLARA, LANDLORD, *and* GUIDE.]

LAND. Will the ladies and gentlemen have something else ?

HOR. Some coffee presently.

OP. Won't the ladies and gentlemen have their pictures taken with the falls for a background ?

INDIAN SALESWOMAN. Will the ladies have any bead-work, moccasins, slippers, belts, caps, lamp-mats, fans, all made by the Indians ?

ANOTHER. Will the ladies and gentlemen see the panorama of the winter views of the falls, grand and imposing ?

HOR. I've no doubt, imposing ; most everything here has been so far.   [TOUTERS *exit.*

MRS. S.   (*To* CLARA, *aside.*)   Clara, the Dooners have gone above the falls to look at the rapids.

CLA. I know it, Aunty.

MRS. S. We waste our time here.   The refusal comes from them.   Our place is there.

CLA. Very well.

MRS. S. Besides, Dooner is lecturing Josephine on the geology of the falls.   He likes us to listen.   From geology to mining is an easy step.   Come.

CLA. My, Aunty, it's so absurd !   [*Exit both.*

WILL. Landlord, give the driver something to drink.

LAND. This way, sir.   [*Both exit round corner.*

HOR. Will, old fellow.

WILL. My dear boy.

HOR. The siege is laid, and we have commenced the attack.

WILL. We came in the same car with the Dooner family.

HOR. At Elmira we were at the same hotel.

WILL. So were the Spoopendykes.

HOR. And again at Rochester.

WILL. So were the Spoopendykes.

HOR. You proposed the Genesee Falls.

WILL. We arrived together at Niagara.

HOR. And every time we met in a new place the papa exclaimed, " What a fortunate coincidence ! "

WILL. Last night you learned that they were going to the Canada side ; this morning you aroused me with the sun like a thoroughbred.

HOR. That's our programme ; hunt the game loyally. Will you join me in an omelette ?

WILL. Thanks, my dear boy. I ought to tell you that at Rochester Miss Dooner looked at me distinctly three times.

HOR. And me, four

WILL. The deuce ! This is getting serious.

HOR. I believe she prefers us both. This may go on a long time before she makes a choice ; luckily, we are men of leisure.

WILL. Ah ! explain how you are able to keep away from your sugar-refinery so long.

HOR. Oh, advantage of partners. One is at Cape May, another at Newport. We have faithful men, and the refinery runs itself. But you, a banker, it appears to me that you travel a great deal.

WILL. Oh, our banking-house doesn't occupy me much. My capital represents me. I am a banker—

HOR. Amateur !

WILL. I haven't, like you, a fall trade that I must get ready for.

HOR. That's so. Therefore, from this on, we make war in earnest.

WILL. Very well. War be it, but like two friends. I had for a moment the idea to yield the place to you ; but I love Josephine seriously.

HOR. I was going to make you the same sacrifice. At Elmira I had half a mind to yield to you and flirt with Clara, but Josephine—

WILL. She is so pretty.

HOR. So sweet.

WILL. So blonde.

HOR. And eyes !

WILL. Just as I love them.

HOR. Therefore I remained.

WILL. You couldn't do otherwise. (*Rises.*)

HOR. Good luck to you. It's a pleasure to have you for an adversary, old fellow.

WILL. My dear Horace! (*Going.*)

HOR. Where are you going?

WILL. No particular place. I think I'll go out and meet the ladies.

HOR. And the coffee.

WILL. I won't take any. Au revoir.   [*Exit* L. N.

HOR. What an excellent boy he is! all heart, all fire; but heart and fire won't fill a man's stomach healthily. He has gone without taking his coffee. Hallo! Waiter!

LAND. Sir.

HOR. The coffee. (*The* LANDLORD *brings it.* HORACE *lights a cigar.*)

LAND. It is served, sir. (HORACE *takes seat at table* R. *and puts one leg on* WILL's *chair.*)

HOR. Bring up that other chair. That will do. (*He puts the other leg up.*) Thanks. Poor Will! He hunts on the go, under the broiling sun, and I—I wait who will reach the goal first. We have the fable of the hare and the tortoise.

LAND. (*Bringing register.*) Sir, would you like to write something in the visitors' book?

HOR. I—I never write after my meals—seldom before. Here we see the delicate and ingenious thoughts of the visitors. (*Reading.*) "It is fine to admire the grandeur of the water, surrounded by your wife. Signed, W. V. Cake, Bakersville." "Surrounded by your wife" is good! "Traveller, pause. Don't forget the Mastodon Harmonists at Brock Hall to-night." Working in a little business. "The view from this side is sublime. Myself and family had our pictures taken in the act of looking at it. Cyrus Thompson, Wheatville." Oh! what stupid donkeys my countrymen are when they travel. (*Cries and tumult without.*)   [MUSIC, *short, hurry.*

LAND. Oh! my heavens!

HOR. What's the matter?

[DOONER *U. L. enters sustained by his wife and the guide and* MRS. SPOOPENDYKE *and* CLARA *and* WILL.]

WILL. Quick. Some brandy!

HOR. What has happened?

JOS. My father barely escaped being drowned.

HOR. Is it possible?

DOON. . (*Seated.*) Caroline, Josephine! Ah! I feel better now.

MRS. S. Thank Heaven!

JOS. (*Giving him the glass.*) Drink! that will do you good.

Doon. Thanks.

Mrs. D. It's all your fault; you ought not to have gone near the rapids.

Doon. I was testing the velocity of the water, when my feet slipped.

Jos. And if Mr. Rittenhouse hadn't caught him in another instant he would have been in the rapids.

Mrs. D. He was there. The rapids were rolling him and bobbing him like a cork. We shrieked for help.

Jos. Then Mr. Willie stretched out his hand.

Cla. With such courage and coolness.

Mrs. D. You are our saviour. Without you my husband, my poor husband, would have gone over the falls to Heaven. (*Weeps.*)

Will. The danger is past. Mrs. Dooner, be calm.

Mrs. D. No. (*Weeping.*) It does me good to cry. You leave the velocity alone, won't you? You don't love us.

Jos. (*To* Will.) Permit me to express to you our deepest thanks. I shall treasure a remembrance of this day all my life. (*Goes to him and takes his hand.*)

Will. Ah! Miss Josephine!

Doon. Yes, yes, Mr. Rittenhouse. No—let me call you Willie.

Will. Why, certainly, Mr. Dooner.

Doon. Willie, give me your hand. I don't know how to express it. But as long as it beats, you will have a place in the heart of Dooner. I can only say that, but what I feel—

Mrs. D. I thank you, Mr. Willie.

Jos. I thank you, Mr. Willie.

Will. Miss Josephine.

Hor. (*Aside.*) I commence to think I did wrong in taking my coffee.

Mrs. S. (*To* Clara.) You will be Mrs. Walbridge, my dear. (*To* Landlord.) You can order our carriage and we will return.

Cla. My, Aunty, it's so absurd! [*Exit with* Mrs. S.

Mrs. D. You can order our carriage and we will return.

Doon. Not at all, my dear. I don't feel the slightest inconvenience from the wet. And I want to go under the falls. They say that's a damp trip, and—

Land. I can give the gentleman some clothes, and dry his own while he goes under the falls.

Doon. Good! Take me to them at once.

Land. This way, sir.

Mrs. D. Come, papa. Au revoir, Mr. Rittenhouse.

Jos. Au revoir, Mr. Rittenhouse.

Doon. Ah, Willie! (*Offering hand.*) While this— No, I'm too wet. [*All four exit into hotel.*

Will. What do you think of that, my dear Horace?

Hor. What can I? It's in the air. You saved the father's life. It wasn't in the programme.

Will. It was a lucky chance.

Hor. The papa calls you Willie, the mother weeps, and the daughter addresses you sentimentally. I am vanquished, it's clear, and I can do nothing but gracefully concede you the victory.

Will. Oh, old fellow, you're joking.

Hor. I joke so little that to-night I leave for Philadelphia.

Will. Indeed!

Hor. Where on your return you will find a friend who wishes you every success.

Will. Thanks.

Hor. One last regret!

Will. Ah, pardon, old fellow. I will not permit you to make this sacrifice.

Hor. Sacrifice? Listen, my dear boy. I do not make you the slightest sacrifice. If I leave the field, it's because I believe I have no chance. And even now, should a chance offer, no matter how small, I remain.

Will. Ah!

Hor. It's strange, since Josephine escapes me, it appears to me that I love her more than ever.

Will. I can understand that; so I will not ask of you the service I had intended.

Hor. What?

Will. No, nothing.

Hor. Speak, I beg.

Will. I had thought, since you were going, to beg you to see Mr. Dooner, and in conversation to touch upon my position and my hopes.

Hor. The deuce!

Will. I can't do it myself. I should have the appearance of claiming a price for the service I rendered him.

Hor. In effect, you want me to ask Josephine's hand for you. That is original, don't you know?

Will. You decline the honor?

Hor. No, Will, I accept.

Will. Thanks, old friend.

Hor. Agree that I am a generous rival. (Dooner's *voice heard.*) I hear the father-in-law. Go, smoke a cigar, and return.

Will. I don't know how to thank you, my dear fellow.

Hor. Take it easy. I shall draw it mild. [Will *exits L. U.*

Doon. (*Enters speaking off.*) Certainly he saved my life, certainly he did. And as long as it beats, the heart of Dooner—I told him.

Hor. Ah, Mr. Dooner, you feel better?

Doon. Very much. I am going to drink three fingers of Can-

ada brandy, and I shall skip down the stairs under the falls.
But where's your friend ?

Hor. He's taking a little walk.

Doon. He's a brave young man. My wife and daughter worship him.

Hor. Oh, when they know him better—a heart of gold, obliging, devoted, and modesty itself.

Doon. Modesty is rare.

Hor. And as he's a banker—he *is* a banker.

Doon. Indeed !

Hor. Partner in the house of Bombax, Traquire & Co. It's flattering to have a fellow's life saved by a banker, eh ? Because he did save your life, eh ! eh ! Without him—

Doon. Certainly, certainly ! It was very genteel in him.

Hor. (*Astonished.*) Genteel ?

Doon. Certainly, quite genteel. You wouldn't underrate the merit of his action, would you ?

Hor. I underrate him ?

Doon. My gratitude will end only with my life. That's it. As long as the heart of Dooner beats. But, between us, the little assistance he gave me was not so great as my wife and my daughter imagine.

Hor. (*Astonished.*) Nonsense !

Doon. Yes, they have got it on the brain. You know these women—

Hor. But when Will caught you, you were rolling in the rapids ?

Doon. I commenced to roll in the rapids, yes, that's true, I rolled, but with a presence of mind astonishing. I perceived an elderberry bush leaning over the water ; I raised my hand, and was just about to grab it when your friend seized me.

Hor. (*Aside.*) Ha, ha ! we shall soon find that he saved his own life.

Doon. Oh, I think none the less of his good intentions. I count on seeing him again, and to reiterate my thanks. I shall invite him some time this winter.

Hor. (*Aside.*) To a cup of tea.

Doon. It appears that this is not the first time that a similar accident has occurred. The landlord tells me that several years since, a gentleman attached to the suite of the Prince of Wales—the Prince—splendid man—belonged to the nobility, was rolling in the same rapids.

Hor. Indeed !

Doon. His driver pulled him out. You see anybody can pull you out. Very well. The baronet—for I think he was a baronet—gave him twenty dollars.

Hor. And very well paid.

Doon. I believe you, for it's worth just about that.

Hor. Not a cent more. (*Aside.*) Oh, but I don't leave for Philadelphia !

Doon. (*Rising.*) Where's the guide ? What keeps our guide ?

Hor. Are the ladies ready ?

Doon. No, they won't go under the falls. But I count upon you.

Hor. And upon Will ?

Doon. If he wishes to be one of us, I shall certainly not refuse the company of Mr. Rittenhouse.

Hor. (*Aside.*) Mr. Rittenhouse ! He's losing his grip. Oh, decidedly, I don't leave for Philadelphia !

Land. (*Enters.*) Sir, the guide is ready. Here are your waterproofs.

Doon. Ah, yes ! It appears that it streams, and that it's slippery down there, and as I don't want to be under any further obligation—

Land. (*Giving the book.*) Will the gentlemen write something in the visitors' book ?

Doon. Certainly. But I wouldn't care to write anything ordinary. I must think of something—a little idea, a pretty thought. (*Giving back book.*) I will dream of it while I'm getting that three fingers of Canada brandy. (*To* Horace.) I am with you in a moment.   [*Exit followed by* Landlord.

Hor. (*Alone.*) The pork-packer is a paragon of ingratitude.

Will. (*Enters.*) Very well ?

Hor. Poor boy !

Will. Have you seen him ?

Hor. Yes.

Will. Have you spoken with him ?

Hor. I have spoken with him.

Will. Then you made my request ?

Hor. No !

Will. No ! Why?

Hor. We promised to be frank. Very well, my dear Willie. I don't leave.

Will. Ah, that makes a difference. May I ask what has changed your determination ?

Hor. Something—or rather the lack of something—and I expect to use it.

Will. Indeed !

Hor. I propose to take another road and arrive quicker.

Will. All right. You are entitled to take it.

Hor. But the tournament continues none the less loyal and amicable.

Will. Yes.

Hor. There's a " yes " a little dry.

Will. (*Giving hand.*) Pardon, Horace, I promise it.

Hor. Fortune favor us !

Doon. (*Entering.*) I am ready. Ah ! Mr. Rittenhouse.

Will. You find yourself recovered from the effects of your wetting ?

Doon. Entirely. Don't speak of the little accident. It is forgotten.

Hor. (*Aside.*) Forgotten, the rapids washed it away.

Doon. We are going under the falls. Are you with us?

Will. I'm a little tired. I'll ask permission to remain here.

Doon. Don't incommode yourself. (*To* Landlord.) Ah, Mr. Landlord, now you may give me the visitors' book. (*Sits and writes.*)

Hor. (*Aside.*) He appears to have found his little thought, his pretty thought.

Doon. (*Reading.*) "How small man, with all his intellect, finds himself, when he stands on this side and looks Niagara in the face!"

Hor. Heavens! that's strong.

Will. (*Aside.*) Flatterer.

Doon. There are men who wouldn't think themselves small standing by the side of Niagara. (*Modestly.*) It isn't the opinion of the whole of mankind.

Hor. (*Aside.*) Neither is the orthography. He has written Niagara Nig-er-y.

Doon. (*To* Landlord, *about to close book.*) Take care. It isn't dry yet.

Land. The guide is ready.

Doon. Forward! Under the falls.

Hor. Forward! [*Both exit with guide down falls.*

Will. What a singular change in the mind of Horace! The ladies are here. They will be out before long. I shall see her. I shall speak to her.

Land. (*Entering.*) This way, sir.

Col. (*Entering.*) I sha'n't stay but a minute. I start directly to take a look at the falls. Order a glass of brandy and water for Colonel Calhoun Bumgartner.

Land. Yes, sir. Colonel Calhoun Baumgartner. [*Exit.*

Col. (*Seeing book.*) Ah, the visitors' book. Let us see. (*Reading.*) "How small man, with all his intellect, finds himself, when he stands on this side and looks Niggery in the face." Behold a gentleman who merits a lesson in spelling." (*Writes in book.*)

Land. (*Enters with glass.*) Ready, sir. A letter for you, sir. (*He pauses near table at* R.)

Col. For me? (*Opens letter.*) Reads: "She didn't shed a tear, O my commander—" (*Hides it, chagrined.*)

Land. Anything else?

Col. (*While writing in book.*) Ah, Mr. Landlord.

Land. Sir.

Col. You don't happen to have among the persons who have stopped with you this morning a visitor named William Rittenhouse?

Will. That is my name, sir.

COL. You, sir, pardon me. (*To* LANDLORD.) Leave us
(*Exit* LANDLORD.) Is it Mr. William Rittenhouse, of the firm
of Bombax, Traquire & Co., Philadelphia, to whom I have the
honor of speaking?

WILL. Yes, sir.

·   COL. I am Colonel Baumgartner, of the Louisiana Tigers
(*Sits and drinks.*)

WILL. Enchanted. But I don't remember to have the advantage of your acquaintance, Colonel.

COL. Indeed. Then permit me to acquaint you with the fact
that you have pursued me out of my country into Canada on account of a check that I had the imprudence to put in circulation.

WILL. A check?

COL. You have obtained a warrant for my arrest.

WILL. It's possible, Colonel. But it is not I; it is the House
who act.

COL. I presume. Very well. I hold no resentment against
you nor your House. I am a bad book-keeper. I thought I had
the money when I drew the check. It appears I had not. Only
permit me to tell you that I didn't leave Philadelphia on account of your warrant.

WILL. I don't doubt it.

COL. On the contrary, as soon as I arrive in Philadelphia in
a fortnight, perhaps sooner, I shall make it known to you, and
I shall be infinitely obliged if you will have me put in Moyamensing just as soon as possible.

WILL. You are using a little pleasantry, Colonel.

COL. Not the least in the world. I ask it of you as a favor.

WILL. I assure you that I don't quite comprehend your idea.

COL. My heavens! I am myself a little embarrassed in explaining. Pardon me, are you a bachelor?

WILL. Yes, Colonel.

COL. Oh, then, I can make my confession. I have the misfortune to have a weakness. I am in love.

WILL. You?

COL. It's very ridiculous, isn't it, at my age?

WILL. I don't say that.

COL. Oh, don't disguise it. I am stuck on a little fool that I
met one evening at a ball in Sansom Street. She is named Ida.

WILL. Ida—I think I know—one.

COL. Probably the same. I thought to amuse myself for a
little while, and now, for three years, she holds me as a cat
does a mouse. She deceives me, she ruins me, she laughs in
my face. I pass my life in buying furniture which she sells the
next day. I want to quit her. I leave. I go to two hundred
places. I arrive at Niagara, and I am not sure that I don't return to Philadelphia to-night. It's stronger than I am. Love
at fifty. You see, it's like the rheumatism, nothing cures it.

WILL. (*Laughing.*) Colonel, I did not need this confidence

to stop the proceedings of my firm. I will write immediately to Philadelphia—

Col. Not at all. Don't write. I want to be imprisoned. It is perhaps a way to cure me of it. I have nothing else left to try.

Will. But, Colonel—

Col. No, imprison me, I beg. The law is in my favor.

Will. Very well, Colonel. As you wish it.

Col. I beg it of you;—instantly, as soon as I return, I will send you my address and you can proceed. I am always at home before ten. (*Bowing. Crosses to* C. L.) Sir, I am happy to have the honor of making your acquaintance.

Will. The honor is mine, Colonel. (*They salute. The* Colonel *exits* L. U. E.) Such is life. He is not half a bad one. (*Seeing* Mrs. D., *who enters.*) Ah, Mrs. Dooner.

Mrs. D. Ah, Mr. Rittenhouse. I thought you had accompanied Mr. Dooner and the gentlemen.

Will. I was under the falls last year, and I asked Mr. Dooner's permission to place mself at your orders.

Mrs. D. Ah, sir! (*Aside.*) He is entirely a man of the world. (*Aloud.*) You admire Niagara very much?

Will. (*Half yawning.*) Oh! it's necessary to go somewhere.

Mrs. D. I wouldn't like to live here always; too much noise and mist. I like quiet. My family is from Bucks County.

Will. Indeed!

Mrs. D. Near Doylestown.

Will. (*Aside.*) We ought to have a correspondent at Doylestown; we have. (*Aloud.*) Are you acquainted with Mr. Pepperhorn at Doylestown?

Mrs. D. (*Surprised.*) Pepperhorn? He's my cousin. Are you acquainted with him?

Will. Intimately. (*Aside.*) I never saw him.

Mrs. D. What a charming man!

Will. Yes, yes.

Mrs. D. It is such a pity that he has his infirmity.

Will. Certainly, it's a great pity.

Mrs. D. Deaf at forty-seven.

Will. (*Aside.*) Oh! he's deaf, our correspondent. That's the reason why he never answers our letters.

Mrs. D. Isn't it singular that a friend of Pepperhorn's should save my husband's life? There are very strange coincidences in the world.

Will. Often also we attribute to coincidence circumstances of which it is entirely innocent.

Mrs. D. (*A little confused.*) Ah! Oh, yes! Often also we attribute— (*Aside.*) What did he try to say?

Will. Thus, madam, our meeting on the cars, and at Elmira, afterward at Rochester, and here. You imagine all that to be mere coincidence?

Mrs. D. In travelling we often meet.

Will. Certainly. And especially when one seeks the other.

Mrs. D. How?

Will. Yes, madam, I can no longer play the comedy of coin-cidence. I owe you the truth on your own account as well as your daughter's.

Mrs. D. My daughter?

Will. You will pardon me. When I first met her I was touched, charmed. I learned that you were going to Niagara, and I—

Mrs. D. You followed us.

Will. Something like it. What could I do? I am in love.

Mrs. D. Mr. Rittenhouse!

Will. Yes, madam, with all the respect, all the discretion that a gentleman owes to a young lady, whom he hopes to be happy enough to make his wife.

Mrs. D. A marriage proposal, and Dooner not here. (*Aloud.*) Certainly, Mr. Rittenhouse, sir, I am charmed, flattered, because your position, your appearance, your education—Pepperhorn— the service you have rendered; but Mr. Dooner is out,—under Niagara Falls, and as soon as he returns—

Jos. (*Enter lively.*) Mamma. (*Stopping.*) Ah, you are con-versing with Mr. Rittenhouse.

Mrs. D. (*Troubled.*) We were conversing—that is, yes. We spoke of Pepperhorn. Mr. Willie knows Pepperhorn. Don't you?

Will. Certainly, I am acquainted with Pepperhorn.

Jos. Oh! how fortunate. Uncle Pepperhorn!

Mrs. D. (*To* Josephine.) My child, how your hair is dressed, and your dress, your collar. (*Low.*) Arrange it.

Jos. (*Astonished.*) What does all this mean? (*Cries and tumult without.* Music. *Hurry.*)

Mrs. D. *and* Jos. Ah! My heavens!

Will. What is it?

[Horace, *sustained by* Dooner *and* Guide, *enter.*]

Doon. (*Very excited.*) Quick, some water, some salt, some vinegar, some brandy!

All. What ails him?

Doon. A terrible accident! Make him drink! Rub his temples!

Hor. Thanks. I feel better.

Will. What has happened to him?

Hor. But for the courage of Mr. Dooner.

Doon. No, no, you mustn't speak. You are not strong enough. (*Recounts.*) It was horrible. We were at the very bottom of the steps under the Falls. Niagara poured above us, calm and majestic—

Hor. (*Aside.*) The boy stood on the burning deck.

Mrs. D. But hurry, tell us.

Jos. Father!

Doon. In an instant. What's the matter? For five minutes we followed each other wrapped in pensive contemplation, Niagara pouring over us, calm and majestic, when suddenly we came upon two steps separated by a deep crevasse slippery with moss. I marched before—

Mrs. D. What imprudence!

Doon. All at once I heard behind me a noise, as though something was falling. I turned. Mr. Wallbridge had disappeared. In an instant I returned. I saw him. He had fallen upon a ledge of rock below. Beyond which the boiling waters seethed to the distant bottom. The very look made me shudder.

Mrs. D. Dooner!

Doon. Then forgetting that I was the father of a family—listening to nothing but his danger—I threw myself—

Mrs. D. and Jos. Heavens!

Doon. Upon my hands and knees I extended my hand to him—he grasped it. I pulled—he pulled—we both pulled. My fears redoubled my strength, and at last we brought him up insensible, once more to the light of the sun, and under the broad blue of the heavens. (*Putting his handkerchief to his face.*)

Jos. O papa!

[Landlord, Photographer, R.; Willie, Horace, C.; Jos., Mrs. D., L.]

Mrs. D. My poor Dooner!

Doon. (*Embracing his wife and daughter.*) Yes, my children, it was a fortunate circumstance.

Will. (*To* Horace.) How do you find yourself?

Hor. (*Low.*) Very well—don't be uneasy. (*Rising.*) Mr. Dooner, you have brought back a son to his mother.

Doon. (*Majestically.*) I have.

Hor. A brother to his sister.

Doon. And a man to society.

Hor. Words lack power to recount such a service.

Doon. They do.

Hor. It is only the heart you understand—the heart—

Doon. Mr. Walbridge. No—let me call you Horace.

Hor. With pleasure. (*Aside.*) Every one in his turn.

Doon. (*Trembling with affection.*) Horace, my friend, my child, your hand. (*Hand.*) I owe to you the sweetest emotions of my life. But for me you would now be a shapeless mass on the rocks beneath the torrent. You owe me all—all. (*Nobility crosses.*) I shall never forget it, never!

Hor. Nor I!

Doon. (*Crosses* R. C.) (*To* Will.) Ah, young man, you don't know the pleasure one feels when he has saved his fellow creature.

Jos. But, papa, he knows it well ; for only just now—

Doon. Ah ! Oh, yes ! That is true. Mister Landlord, bring me the visitor's book.

[WILLIE R. *corner.*]

Mrs. D. What for ?

Doon. Before quitting these scenes I desire to consecrate by a sentiment the remembrance of this event.

Land. Here it is, sir.

Doon. Thanks—Hai ! What is this ? Who wrote this ?

All. What ?

Doon. (*Write this in book.*) (*Reading.*) I desire to observe to Mr. Dooner that if he wants to look niggery in the face he needs another g, but if he means Niagara, one or two a's will do as well. Signed, Col. Baumgartner. [JOSEPHINE *crosses down* R. C. *to* DOON.

All. Hai ! What ?

Jos. (*Low to* DOON.) Yes, papa, Niagara has not a y at the end.

Doon. I know it. I will answer this gentleman. (*Writing.*) (*Reading.*) The Col. is a jackass. Signed, Dooner. (*It rains.*)

Land. The carriage is ready.

Doon. Let us start. Gentlemen, if you will accept a place. (*Both bow.*)

Mrs. D. (*Umbrella.*) (*Calling* DOONER *aside.*) Dooner, assist me with my shawl. (*Low.*) Some one proposed to marry Josephine.

Doon. Hai ! So they did to me also.

Mrs. D. It was Mr. Willie Rittenhouse.

Doon. My man was Horace—my friend Horace.

Mrs. D. But it appears to me that Willie—

Doon. We will talk of it later.

Jos. My ! how it rains !

Doon. The deuce ! How many will the carriage hold ?

Land. Four inside, and one with the driver.

Doon. That's just the number.

Will. Don't inconvenience yourselves for me.

Doon. Horace, take a seat with us.

Jos. (*Low to* DOONER.) And Mr. Rittenhouse ?

Doon. My heavens ! there are only four seats. He can sit with the driver.

Jos. In such a rain ?

Mrs. D. A man who saved your life.

Doon. I will lend him the umbrella.

Jos. Ah !

Doon. Come, come ! All aboard !

Hor. (*Aside.*) No, I don't leave for Philadelphia. Not much !

[*Enter from all sides* TOUTERS. *Won't the ladies buy, etc. Will the gentlemen, etc.*]

Op. (*With camera.*) Won't the gentlemen have their pictures taken in the rain, with Falls for a background ?

[*The speeches and action of the* TOUTERS *are simultaneous, to make curtain lively.*]

CURTAIN.

ACT III.

SCENE.—PARLOR AT DOONER'S, RICHLY FURNISHED, *doors* R. & L. & C. *Also* L. 1st C. D. *is main entrance from hall, from street, to dining-room and* C. *Door* R., *apartment of the* SPOOPEN-DYKES. *Door* L., *apartment of* MRS. D., *with* JOSEPHINE'S *beyond. Door* L. *first leads to* DOONER'S *Library. Chairs, sofas, ornaments, etc. Table* C., *with writing materials and card-receiver on it.*

ALICE. (*Alone, sitting in a chair.*) A quarter to twelve to-day Mr. Dooner returns from his trip with his wife and daughter. I received a letter from him yesterday. Here it is. Long Branch, August 24th. Sweep out, dust and air the rooms. (*Speaks.*) It is done. (*Reads.*) Tell Mammy, the cook, to have dinner ready for us. Tell her to make some snapper soup, and as we have had nothing but hotel dinners for this long time, tell her to buy a couple of woodcock. See that they are quite fresh. If the woodcock are too dear, let her get a loin of veal with onions. (*Speaks.*) Mr. Dooner can come : everything is ready. Here are his papers, his letters ; the cards of all the callers. Ah, there came this morning early a gentleman whose acquaintance is new to us. He told me his name was Colonel—Colonel (*Reads card.*) Bungstarter, there's a name for you. He can pass anywhere. (*Bell rings.*) Ah the bell. It's Dooner, I know his ring.

[*Enter* DOONER, MRS. DOONER, *and* JOSEPHINE, *carrying their parcels and bags.* MRS. SPOOPENDYKE *and* CLARA.]

DOON. Here we are, Alice.

AL. Ah, sir ! Mrs. Dooner ! Miss Josephine ! (*Takes their things.*)

DOON. Ah, but it's sweet to return home again. Sweet home, be it ever so. Welcome, welcome ! Alice, did you get the mosquito bar out ?

AL. Yes, sir.

MRS. D. We ought to have been home a week ago.

DOON. Long Branch led to Asbury Park, and Ocean Grove let us out. Has any one called expecting us ?

(MRS. DOONER *shows* MRS. SPOOPENDYKE *and* CLARA *into room right.*) This way, Mrs. Spoopendyke. [*Exit all three.*

AL. Yes, sir. The cards are on the table.

DOON. (*Taking cards, reads.*) Ah ! Will. Rittenhouse.

JOS. (*With joy.*) Oh ! Mr. Rittenhouse !

[MRS. DOONER *returns.*]

DOON. (*Reading other cards.*) Horace Walbridge—charming young man. Will. Rittenhouse and Horace Walbridge. Magnificent young man, Will. Rittenhouse.

AL. The young men have been here every day to inquire.

MRS. D. You owe them a visit.

DOON. Certainly—I shall call on him ; my splendid Horace !

JOS. And Mr. Rittenhouse.

DOON. I shall go to see him also, later. (*Rises.*)

JOS. (*To* ALICE.) Help me to carry in these pictures.

AL. Yes, Miss. (*Regarding* DOONER.) Sir, you have grown stouter. It's easy to see you've had a fine trip.

DOON. Splendid, Alice, splendid. Ah, you don't know. I saved a man's life.

AL. (*Incredulous.*) O sir ! Mr. Docner ! Nonsense !

[*Exit with* JOSEPHINE L.

DOON. Hai, nonsense ! She's a fool.

MRS. D. Now that we have returned, I hope you will decide between these young men. Two young men are one too many.

DOON. I haven't changed my mind. I like Horace better.

MRS. D. Why ?

DOON. I don't know why. I find him more—in fact, he pleases me.

MRS. D. But the other, Willie, saved your life.

DOON. He saved my life. The same old story.

MRS. D. What have you to object to in him ? His family is honorable ; his position excellent.

DOON. My heavens ! I don't object to anything particularly. I don't care anything about him.

MRS. D. It only lacked that !

DOON. You see I find him a little overbearing.

MRS. D. What ? Mr. Rittenhouse overbearing ?

DOON. He has the tone of a protector—a sort of I'll-take-care-of-you style. It seems to me that he never forgets the little service that he rendered.

MRS. D. The other repeats without cessation. "Oh, but for you ! Ah, but for you !" That flatters your vanity, and that is why you prefer him.

DOON. Me—vanity ! I have perhaps the right to be vain.

MRS. D. Oh !

DOON. Yes, madam, the man who has risked his life to save his fellow-creature may well be proud of himself. But I prefer to maintain a modest silence. A style characteristic of true courage.

MRS. D. But that doesn't prevent Mr. Rittenhouse—

DOON. Josephine doesn't love him. She can't love him.

MRS. D. What do you know about it ?

DOON. Oh, I suppose—

MRS. D. There is one way to ascertain, and that is to question her. And we will agree on the one she prefers.

Doon. Good! All right! But don't influence her.

Mrs. D. Here she is. (JOSEPHINE *enters* L. *and comes down* L. *of* DOONER.) Josephine, my dear child, we want to speak to you seriously.

Jos. To me?

Doon. Yes.

Mrs. D. You are now at an age to marry. Two young gentleman have presented themselves and asked for your hand. Both are satisfactory. But we don't wish to control your choice, and we have resolved to leave you at liberty to make your own.

Jos. How so?

Doon. You pick and choose yourself.

Mrs. D. One of the young men is Mr. Willie Rittenhouse.

Jos. (*Pleased.*) Ah! Indeed!

Doon. (*Quick.*) Don't influence her.

Mrs. D. The other is Mr. Horace Wallbridge.

Doon. A charming young man, distinguished, spirituelle, and who, I do not hesitate to say, has all my sympathies.

Mrs. D. But you are influencing her.

Doon. Not at all. I state a fact. Now you are free. Choose!

Jos. You embarrass me very much. Which do you prefer?

Doon. No, no. Choose yourself.

Mrs. D. Speak, my child.

Jos. Very well; since it's absolutely necessary to make a choice, I prefer Mr. Rittenhouse.

Mrs. D. There!

Doon. Rittenhouse! Why not Horace?

Jos. But Mr. Rittenhouse saved your life, papa.

Doon. There it goes again. It's tiresome. My heavens!

Mrs. D. Very well. You see it's no use hesitating longer.

Doon. Ah, but permit me, my dear wife, a father cannot thus lightly throw off his obligations! I will reflect. I will make some inquiries.

Mrs. D. Mr. Dooner, that's not keeping faith.

Doon. Caroline!

[MRS. SPOOPENDYKE *and* CLARA *return* R., *having removed wraps.*]

CLA. We are charmed with our rooms, Mrs. Dooner. (*Bow and smile.*)

[HUCKLESTONE *and* ALICE *enter.*]

AL. Come in—they have just arrived.

Doon. Hello! It's Hucklestone!

HUCK. (*Bowing.*) I learned that you were coming to-day. Therefore, I demanded leave of absence. I said that I was sick.

Doon. My dear friend, that's very kind. (*Introducing.* MRS. SPOOPENDYKE, MISS CLARA.) You dine with us. We have some woodcock.

Huck. Well, if I'm not in the way—

Al. (*Low to* Dooner.) It's veal and onions. [*Exit.*

Doon. Ah! (*To* Huck.) Well, never mind. Your excuse is sufficient. Another time.

Huck. (*Aside. Others up.*) How, my excuse? If he thinks that I want his dinner. (*Taking* Dooner *aside.*) I came to speak o you about the $300 you lent me the day you left.

Doon. (*Glad.*) Ah, you have come to pay me, eh?

Huck. No: I don't touch my salary till to-morrow—but at noon precisely.

Doon. Oh, that doesn't press!

Huck. Excuse me, I want it paid.

Doon. Ah, you must know I bought you a present.

Huck. A present for me?

[Mrs. D. *on the* R., *standing, faces off and up, busy at a stand or etagere, but turns quickly for her speeches.* Josephine, *similar business,* L. U. S. *The others seated. The adventure is told with gusto and spirit, each one apparently trying to have a word.*]

[Cla., Doon., Huck., Mrs. S.]

Doon. Oh, a little something to show that we thought of you while we were away. When we were at Niagara on the Canada side I bought a pin-cushion and a smoking-cap, all of velvet and bead-work, made by the Indians. Oh, lovely! Then I heard that kid gloves were a gift on that side, so I bought a dozen of kid gloves—beauties. I said, the cushion is for the cook; the lamp-mat for Alice, and the gloves for my old friend Hucklestone.

Huck. (*Aside.*) Of course I come after the servants. (*Aloud.*) Well.

Mrs. S. Our driver seemed a very nice fellow, only a lit-.le too full of fun. The moment we started for the American side, he commenced to tell us to look out for the Custom House officers. You know he (*indicating* Dooner) is the soul of honor in business, but he didn't want to pay any duties on such little things as them.

Doon. The driver talked as though it would cost about $25. So I drove back to the Canada Hotel, went up to a room and stuck the pin-cushion in the top of my hat.

Huck. And the gloves?

Doon. I put them in my bosom under my wrapper.

Huck. That was a good idea.

Doon. Wasn't it? Well, as soon as we got in the carriage, that driver began about the Custom House duties again.

Mrs. S. He said they came and asked questions of all carriages, but if a man was on foot nothing was said to him.

Doon. The day was awful hot, and he said so much about it that I got nervous and anxious.

MRS. D. I asked him where the cushion and mat were. He
told me that he had sent them by express.

DOON. You see I didn't want to let her know, you know.

HUCK. No ; of course not.

DOON. Well, I got so nervous, that when we got in the mid-
dle of the suspension bridge I told the driver that I thought I
would get out and walk over, so that I could see the rapids
better.   .

HUCK. And walk past the Custom House ?

ALL. Of course. (*Smiling.*)

DOON. Yes ; the driver grinned.

MRS. S. Away we went, and he followed on foot.

DOON. Oh, how hot it was ! There I was, way up above Niagara River. The wind blowing. I pulled my hat with the
pin-cushion down on to my head, and I felt as though I was
walking a tight-rope for my life. I tell you, Hucklestone, how I
did wish that pincushion and mat were in Africa. The gloves,
I knew, were safe.

HUCK. Yes, they were safe.

MRS. S. Well, when we got near the shore there was the Custom House right at the end of the bridge.

DOON. So I sauntered up to one of the piers, leaned against it,
kind a off-hand, and gazed up the river as though to drink in
the scene.

HUCK. That was cool.

DOON. Wasn't it ? Well, what do you suppose the devil of
a driver did.

HUCK. What was it ?

MRS. S. We drove just beyond the Custom House and stopped.
The Custom House officer came up to the carriage, asked if
we had anything dutiable ; we said no, and he went away.

DOON. You would have supposed that fool of a driver would
have gone on—no—

HUCK. Stupid !

MRS. S. There was a railroad depot there, with a lot of countrymen standing around, and they all came up staring at us.

DOON. Then that driver commenced his funny business.

MRS. S. He called it fooling the gawks. He said, It is strange
what a pitch they have brought science to. They almost make
a human being. Now, you see that man there.

MRS. D. I turned to look and he pointed to Dooner.

MRS. S. He's got a wax nose and you can't discover it. He's
got a tin ear and yet you can't tell it from the other one.

MRS. D. We thought it was a good joke.

DOON. Heavens, what a joke ! The crowd all started for me.
I was standing there gazing at the prospect, and trying to look
unconcerned, while the cushion, mat, and gloves were eating
into my vitals.

ALL. Ha, ha !

Doon. Imagine, they came down, walked around me all the
time, gazing stealthily at me. I took them for revenue officers,
and as they pried and winked, trying to detect the wax nose
and tin ear, the perspiration poured from me in streams.

Mrs. D. There they kept him suffering the torments of the
condemned.

Doon. Until a puff of wind blew my hat with the cushion
and mat into the river. Of course they laughed, and I broke -
away and got into the carriage.

Huck. But you had the gloves safe.

Doon. Yes, I had the gloves safe.

All. He had the gloves safe. (*Smiling.*)

Doon. I hurried up-stairs to my room. I threw open my col-
lar, unbuttoned my under-wrapper, and pulled them out.
Then, Oh, the heat I had suffered ! That tin-ear perspiration !
Hucklestone, the gloves were—

All. Boiled ! (*All rise, laughing.*)

Huck. I thank you all the same, hi ! hi ! I like my gloves
boiled. (*Aside.*) He might have been man enough to pay the
duties.

Doon. The next day I received a letter from the Custom
House officer. " Sir, what was in your hat before it blew off ?"
Without a moment's hesitation I answered, " Sir, my head !"

Huck. That was good !

Doon. Wasn't it ? He wrote back, " Sir, timber is dutiable," inferring—

All. Ha ! ha !

Mrs. S. That he was a blockhead.

All. Ha ! ha !

Doon. I immediately responded, " Sir, you are a meddlesome
puppy." Signed, " Cadwallader Dooner."

Huck. That was rash.

Doon. Yes, I regretted it. He answered, " Sir, you have at-
tempted to defraud the government ; you will hear from me."

Huck. You will, Custom House inspectors are severe.

Doon. Well, no matter. Caroline, show Hucklestone the
boiled gloves.

Jos. Mr. Hucklestone, you shall see my pictures.

[*Exit* Mrs. Dooner, Josephine, Hucklestone, *and* Clara l.]

Mrs. S. At last I have a chance. Now for Clara and the new
mine.

Doon. Hucklestone is a good fellow, he is very fond of me.
But he don't like the gloves a bit.

Mrs. S. Pardon my alluding to it, my dear Mr. Dooner. Two
young gentlemen are now paying attentions to your daughter.

Doon. Well, madam, yes, somewhat.

Mrs. S. One of them has been paying particular attention to
my niece.

Doon. Which one, madam, which one ?

Mrs. S. It is the one you have decided to refuse.

Doon. But I haven't quite decided which one to refuse.

Mrs. S. That doesn't matter ; it's the one you will refuse.

Doon. Oh, she wants the one that's left !

Mrs. S. The poor girl's heart is set on him.

Doon. I don't exactly know which him—but—

Mrs. S. We may depend on your good services.

Doon. You may, madam, you may.

Mrs. S. Thank you so much. Now, I have something else of equal importance to myself to propose. (*Both sit.*)

Doon. (*Sits.*) Oh, you want me to look up somebody for you, eh ? My dear madam !

Mrs. S. No, Mr. Dooner. I am content to remain a widow, fancy free, except for the very warm regard I have for you, my good friend, Mr. Dooner.

Doon. O Mrs. Spoopendyke !

Mrs. S. I have such a profound admiration for your business qualifications.

Doon. I, ah ! would not be vain. But my opinion on pork was asked by the War Department.

Mrs. S. I want to direct your attention to the argentiferous lode.

Doon. How much of a load ?

Mrs. S. I want you to become interested in Baby Mine.

Doon. Oh, Mrs. Spoopendyke ! I really—which one ?

Mrs. S. The new one.

Doon. The—oh !

Mrs. S. The one just started.

Doon. Why, Mrs. Spoopendyke !

Mrs. S. Mr. Dooner, I look upon you as a part proprietor of it.

Doon. Me—oh—I—Mrs. Spoopendyke. You really can't mean—

Mrs. S. Yes, my dear sir. I consider you as in on the ground floor.

Doon. Mrs. S.—I—What will Mrs. Dooner say ?

Mrs. S. She, oh, she doesn't give attention to such matters.

Doon. Oh, but, my dear madam, she does ! I can't even mention Emma without her boiling with rage.

Mrs. S. Emma ! what Emma ? Not Little Emma ?

Doon. I—well, yes, little Emma.

Mrs. S. You don't really mean to say that you have been weak enough to throw money away on Little Emma ?

Doon. Well, yes. Not much, not much.

Mrs. S. Well, sir, you mustn't think that everything is such a swindle as Little Emma.

Doon. I hope not.

Mrs. S. Here is something that will enable you to get even.

Doon. I should like to get even on little Emma. What ?

Mrs. S. Why, my dear sir. Don't you understand, on the darling new Baby Mine ?

Doon. Oh !

Mrs. S. It fairly boils over with alluvial.

Doon. Soothing syrup, madam, soothing syrup.

Mrs. S. It assays 42 to the ton.

Doon. What ? How much baby ?

Mrs. S. We assayed four tons of the Baby lode.

Doon. Heavens ! Four tons of babies !

Mrs. S. Four tons of babies ! (*They rise.*) Mr. Dooner, I am speaking of the Baby Mine.

Doon. Oh, a mine !

Mrs. S. Our new silver mine, and I want you to take 30,000 shares on the ground floor.

Doon. 30,000 shares. My goodness ! How much a share ?

Mrs. S. Four-cents, first call.

Doon. I subscribe, madam, I subscribe. (*Aside.*) Baby Mine.

Mrs. S. Oh, thank you, thank you, dear Mr. Dooner, so much ! It will be well watered by and by. (*Starting* R.)

Doon. Watered, the oh—yes, yes, its stock.

Mrs. S. And you won't forget Clara, will you ?

Doon. Clara—Oh, for the one that's left! No, I won't forget Clara.

Mrs. S. Thank you, Mr. Dooner. You dear Mr. Dooner, so much. 　　　　　　　　　　　　　　　　　　　　　[*Exit* R.

Doon. The Baby Mine.

[HUCK, Mrs. DOONER, *and* JOSEPHINE *return.*]

Al. (*Announcing, enters.*) ·Mr. Will. Rittenhouse.

Jos. Ah !

Mrs. D. Welcome, Mr. Rittenhouse. We are delighted to see you.

Will. (*Bowing.*) Madam, Mr. Dooner.

Doon. Enchanted, enchanted ! (*Aside.*) He always has that style, the air of the protector.

Mrs. D. Introduce him to Mr. Hucklestone.

Doon. Certainly. Hucklestone, permit me to introduce to you Mr. Willie Rittenhouse, one of our travelling acquaintances.

Jos. (*Lively.*) He saved papa's life.

Doon. (*Aside.*) There it goes again.

Huck. How—your life was in danger ?

Doon. No—a little.

Will. Not worth the trouble of repeating.

Doon. (*Aside.*) Always his little air.

Al. (*Announcing.*) Mr. Horace Wallbridge.

[*Enter* HORACE.]

Doon. (*Enthusiastic.*) Ah, here he is, my dear friend, my good Horace ! (*Meeting him.*)

Hor. (*Saluting.*) Good-morning, ladies. Good-morning, Will.

Doon. (*Taking his arm.*) Come, let me present to you Mr. Hucklestone. Hucklestone, I want to introduce you to one of my friends—one of my best friends, Mr. Horace Wallbridge.

Huck. Mr. Wallbridge of the sugar refinery.

Hor. (*Bowing.*) We are somewhat acquainted.

Doon. Ah, if it hadn't been for me he wouldn't pay you your salary to-morrow.

Huck. Why?

Doon. (*With style.*) Why, simply because I saved his life, my good friend.

Huck. You? (*Aside.*) They appear to have passed their time saving each other's lives.

Doon. (*Recounting.*) We were under the falls; Niagara poured over our heads, tranquil and majestic.

Hor. (*Aside.*) The burning deck again.

Doon. We followed each other, slowly, silently, wrapped in pensive contemplation—

Jos. (*Who has been opening journal.*) Ah, papa! Who do you think is in the newspaper? You are.

Doon. How, am I in the newspaper?

Jos. (*Giving paper.*) Read it yourself, there.

Doon. Now I shall find that I am drawn on the grand jury again. (*Reading.*). A correspondent writes us from Niagara—

All. Hilo! Ah!

Doon. (*Reads.*) " An accident, which would have been fol-lowed by the most deplorable consequences occurred under the falls on the Canada side. Mr. Horace Wallbridge missed his footing and fell upon one of the slippery ledges of rocks just over the boiling chasm below. In a moment more he would have been dashed into eternity, but Mr. Dooner, a Philadelphia merchant of widespread repute, most favorably known in his own city, who was with the party, at the risk of his life, threw himself over the ledge." (*Speaks.*) That's the fact. " And after prodigious efforts he was enabled to rescue his companion. Such admirable courage is worthy of universal acknowledgement and the esteem of all will follow him for his generous hardihood."

All. Oh!

Hor. (*Aside.*) Twenty cents a line.

Doon. *Repeating.*) Such admirable courage is worthy of uni-versal acknowledgment—and the esteem.—(*To* Horace.) My friend, my son.

Hor. (*Aside.*) Decidedly I'm on the winner.

Doon. Certainly I'm no politician. but I express my opinion freely and openly. There's some good in newspapers yet. (*Putting paper in his pocket.* (*Aside.*) I must buy ten copies.

Mrs. D. Cadwallader, if we should send the newspapers the account of Mr. Willie's splendid rescue.

Jos. Oh, yes. That would make a fitting finish to the ac-count.

Doon. No, no. It's unnecessary. I don't want to occupy the papers too much with my private affairs.

[*Enter* ALICE.]

AL. Sir, an officer just left this summons for you.

MRS. D. (*Alarmed.*) A summons!

Doon. Have no fear, my dear, I owe nothing to nobody, on the contrary, others owe me.

HUCK. (*Aside.*) He said that for me.

Doon. (*Eying it.*) A summons before the United States Court for an attempt to defraud the revenue.

ALL. Oh, my heavens!

WILL. What does it mean?

Doon. A Custom House officer, who went after my hat. I was a little too quick; I called him a meddlesome puppy.

HUCK. That's very grave, very grave.

Doon. What?

HUCK. An attempt to defraud the revenue when it's found out.

Doon. Eh?

HUCK. From one to five years in prison.

ALL. In prison!

Doon. What, after fifty years of a life pure and without reproach, I am to be placed in the criminals' dock? Never, never!

HUCK. (*Aside.*) That will teach him to pay the duties on his presents.

Doon. (*Troubled.*) Ah, my friends! What can I do?

MRS. D. We will see. Be calm, Cadwallader.

JOS. My poor papa!

HOR. Have courage.

WILL. Wait, I can perhaps get you out of this.

ALL. Ah!

Doon. You, my friend—my good friend!

WILL. I am intimately acquainted with a high official in the Custom House. I will go and see him. Perhaps we can induce the Niagara man to withdraw his complaint.

HUCK That appears to me to be difficult.

WILL. Why? There seems to be nothing but calling him a name—

Doon. Which I regret.

WILL. Give me the summons. I think it can be arranged. Don't let it torment you, my dear Mr. Dooner.

Doon. (*Taking his hand.*) Ah, Horace! (*Remembering.*) No, Willie—Hold! Let me embrace you. (*Bows.*)

JOS. Oh, how fortunate! (*Going up with* MRS. DOONER.)

WILL. (*To* HORACE.) It's my turn. Now I am on the winner.

HOR. So it seems. (*Aside.*) I thought I had it all my own way.

HUCK. I will take my leave.

DOON. Are you going to leave us ?

HUCK. Yes. (*Dryly.*) I dine in the city. [*Exit with* WILLIE.

MRS. D. (*Approaches.   Low.*) Very well.   What do you think of Mr. Rittenhouse now ?

DOON. He ? He's an angel.

MRS. D. And you hesitate to give your consent ?

DOON. I hesitate no longer.

MRS. D. Very good. I will leave you.   There remains nothing but to acquaint Mr. Wallbridge with our decision.

DOON. Oh, the poor boy !   Do you think it necessary ?

MRS. D. Certainly. You don't want to keep him longer in suspense ?

DOON. Oh, no !   You are right.

MRS. D. I leave you with him.   Courage ! (*Aloud.*)   Come, Josephine.   (*Bowing.*).   Mr. Wallbridge.

[*Exit with* JOSEPHINE L.

HOR. (*Aside.*)   I am evidently losing ground.

DOON. Brave young man.   It pains me, but I must.   (*Aloud.*) My dear Horace.   My good Horace, I have a painful communication to make to you.

HOR. Now we get it.

DOON. You have done me the honor to ask the hand of my daughter.   I should have been delighted to have you for a son, but circumstances—events— Your friend Willie has rendered me such important services—

HOR. I understand.

DOON. Because every one says he saved my life.

HOR. But the little elderberry bush which you were going to grasp—

DOON. Certainly the little elderberry bush, but it was very little, and it might have broken, and as I didn't get hold of it—

HOR. Certainly.

DOON. No, but that is not all.   At this very moment that excellent young man is running through the city to get me out of this Cus—Custom House trouble.   I owe him the honor— the honor.

HOR. Mr. Dooner, the sentiments that you express are too noble for me to oppose them.

DOON. True, you wouldn't have me—

HOR. I remember nothing but your courage, your devotion to me.

DOON. (*Shaking hand.*)   Ah, Horace ! (*Aside.*)   It's astonishing how I love that young man.

HOR. Also, before bidding you farewell—

DOON. Hai ?

HOR. Before leaving you.

DOON. How ?   Are you going to leave us ?   Why ?

HOR. I could not continue visits which would be compromising to Miss Josephine, your daughter, and which could not be otherwise than painful to me.

Doon. Come. Nonsense! The only young man that I ever saved.

Hor. But your image will never leave me. I have formed a project. It is to fix upon canvas, as it is already upon my heart, the heroic scene at Niagara.

Doon. A picture! You want to put me in a picture?

Hor. I have already addressed one of our most illustrious painters upon the subject—one of those who work for posterity.

Doon. Posterity! Ah, Horace! (*Aside.*) It's extraordinary how I love that young man.

Hor. I want above all the portrait exact.

Doon. Certainly, certainly. That's what I should prefer myself.

Hor. It will be necessary for you to give five or six sittings to the artist.

Doon. Of course, certainly. My dear friend, twenty, thirty. I won't tire. We will sit together.

Hor. Ah, no! Not I.

Doon. Why?

Hor. Because this is the way I have conceived the picture. You see on the canvas only Niagara.

Doon. (*Uneasy.*) Very well, and what about me?

Hor. Niagara and you.

Doon. Ah, that's it. I and Niagara, tranquil and majestic. But you. Where will you be?

Hor. On the ledge below—out of sight. You see nothing but my two hands clasped and suppliant.

Doon. What a magnificent picture!

Hor. We will place it at the academy.

Doon. Ah, yes. At the Academy of Fine Arts.

Hor. And we will inscribe upon the frame these words—

Doon. No, no buncombe. No extravagant praise. We will place on it simply the article from my newspaper— A correspondent writes us from Niagara—

Hor. That's a little dry.

Doon. Yes; but we will arrange it. (*With emotion.*) Ah, Horace, my son. (*Aside.*) It's extraordinary how I do love that young man!

Hor. Adieu, Mr. Dooner. We shall seldom see each other now.

Doon. No, impossible, it's impossible. This marriage— Nothing is decided yet.

Hor. But—

Doon. Stay, I wish it.

Hor. (*Aside.*) The winner comes our way again.

Al. (*Enters and to announce.*) Colonel Calhoun Bungstarter.

Doon. (*Astonished.*) Who the deuce is he?

Col. (*Entering.*) Pardon me, gentlemen. I disturb you perhaps.

Doon. Not at all, sir.

Col. (*To* Horace.) Is this Mr. Dooner, whom I have the honor of addressing?

Doon. I am that gentleman, sir.

Col. (*To* Dooner.) Ah, sir, I have been looking for you for a fortnight. I have already visited a dozen places, there are so many Dooner's in Philadelphia; but I am tenacious.

Doon. (*Showing chair.*) You have something to communicate to me. (*He sits.* Horace *goes up.*)

Col. (*Sitting.*) I don't know yet. Permit me first to ask you a question. Are you the gentleman who made within a month a trip to Niagara Falls?

Doon. Yes, sir, the same. I believe I may say, "I am the man."

Col. Then it was you who wrote upon the hotel register, "The Colonel is a jackass."

Doon. How—you are—

Col. Yes, sir, I am the Colonel.

Doon. (*Saluting.*) Delighted!

Hor. (*Coming down. Aside.*) The deuce! The horizon grows obscure.

Col. Mr. Dooner, sir. I am neither quarrelsome nor disputatious, but I do not permit any one to take such liberties with my name.

Doon. But you wrote on the same book more than a lively note in relation to me.

Col. I! I am obliged to state that Niagara does not terminate with a y. Look at the dictionary.

Doon. Very well, sir; but you are not obliged to correct my pretended mistakes in orthography. Why did you meddle with it?

Col. Pardon me, sir, the language of my country is about the only thing I have left in it—a language, grand, sonorous, a little peculiar sometimes in the spelling, as you know.

Doon. I!

Col. And when I encounter it in another country, under another flag, I am bound to protect it, and to protest against those who mean to be read "Niagara" and write "Niggery."

Doon. So, sir, are you going to have the pretensions to give me a lesson?

Col. The idea is far from me.

Doon. Luckily for you sir. (*Aside.*) He wilts.

Col. But without wishing to give you a lesson, I come to demand of you, politely, an explanation.

Doon. (*Aside.*) He's a livery-stable Colonel.

Col. Two things. First, if you persist—

Doon. I don't want your reasons. You imagine you can intimidate me, sir. My courage has been proven, do you understand, and you shall see it exemplified.

Col. That is sufficient. Where?

Doon. At the Academy of Fine Arts next season.

Col. Oh, permit me. It will be impossible for me to wait until then. To come to the point; do you take back your words—yes or no?

Doon. Nothing of the kind, sir.

Col. Be careful.

Hor. (*Comes down l.*) (*Soothing, advisory.*) Mr. Dooner.

Doon. Nothing whatever. (*Aside.*) He amounts to nothing but his whiskers.

Col. (*Rising.*) Then, Mr. Dooner, I shall have the honor to wait for you to-morrow at noon precisely, with my second and a surgeon, in the woods near Strawberry Hill.

Hor. Colonel, one word. (*Ready to ring bell l.*)

Col. We will wait for you near the mansion.

Hor. But, Colonel—

Col. A thousand pardons. I have an appointment with a dealer to choose some furniture. To-morrow noon. (*Bowing.*) Gentlemen, I have the honor. [*Exit.*

Hor. The deuce! You are well mixed up, with a Colonel, too.

Doon. He a Colonel! Nonsense! Do genuine Colonels amuse themselves correcting mistakes in orthography?

Hor. No matter. It's necessary to inquire—to find out—(*He rings.*) To know with whom we are dealing.

Al. (*Enters.*) Sir.

Doon. Why did you admit that man who just left?

Al. He had already been here, sir, this morning. I forgot to give you his card.

Hor. Ah, his card!

Doon. Give it. (*Reading.*) Calhoun Baumgartner, Ex-Colonel Louisiana Tigers.

Hor. Louisiana Tigers!

Doon. Thunder and Mars!

Al. What's the matter?

Doon. Nothing. Leave us. [*Exit ALICE.*

Hor. Jiminy! This is a pretty situation.

Doon. What can I do? I was a little too quick—a man so polite. I took him for a confidence man.

Hor. What shall we do?

Doon. It will be necessary to find some way of—(*idea strikes.*) Ah!

Hor. What?

Doon. Nothing—nothing. There is no way. I have insulted him, and I must fight him. (*Starting left.*) Good-by.

Hor. Where are you going?

Doon. To put my affairs in order. You understand.

Hor. But is there no way ?

Doon. Horace, when the hour of danger sounds, you will not see Dooner weaken.   [*Exit* L.

Hor. Here's a pretty mess. But it's impossible. I can't permit Mr. Dooner to fight with a Louisiana Tiger. But he's got courage, the father-in-law. And on the other side the Colonel. Uh ! And all that for not spelling Niagara right. Let's see. If I can notify the police—and—no. But why not ? I have no other choice. No one will know about it. (*He takes pen and paper, sitting.*) A letter to the Chief of Police. (*Writing.*) Sir, I have the honor to inform you. (*Speaking while writing.*) Send an officer to the point named. It will prevent possible bloodshed. (*Folds letter.*) Now I must find some one to carry it. Alice can arrange it. Alice ! Alice !

[*He exits, calling,* C.

[Dooner *enters alone, holding letter.*]

Doon. Chief of Police—Sir, it is my duty to inform you that two desperate men intend to exchange shots to-morrow at a quarter before twelve. (*Speaks.*) I put it a quarter before, so they would be on time. (*Reading.*) At a quarter before twelve, in the woods on Strawberry Hill. It belongs to you to protect the lives of our citizens. One of the combatants is a well-known merchant, father of a family, a devoted friend of the city government, and very influential in his ward. Do not permit him to put his life in jeopardy. Now the address. (*Writes.*) Very pressing—important. Now where is Alice ?

[Horace *enters with letter.*]

Hor. Impossible to find the servant. (*Seeing* Dooner, *hides letter.*) Oh !

Doon. (*Seeing* Horace, *hides letter.*) Horace ?

Hor. Well, Mr. Dooner !

Doon. You see I am calm—like bronze. (*Perceiving* Mrs. Dooner *and* Josephine *enter* L.) My wife, silence !

Mrs. D. My dear Cadwallader, Josephine's piano teacher has sent us some tickets for a concert to-morrow. Matinée.

Doon. (*Aside.*) Matinée !

Mrs. D. It is his benefit. Will you accompany us ?

Doon. Impossible. To-morrow, my dear, I shall be busy.

Mrs. D. But you have nothing to do.

Doon. Yes, I have some business—very important—ask Mr. Walbridge.

Hor. Very important.

Mrs. D. What a serious air. Your face is as long as a horse's. I might think you were afraid of something.

Doon. Me afraid ? You should see me on the field of honor.

Mrs. D. The field of honor !

Doon. (*Aside.*) By George ! that slipped out.

Jos. (*Flying to him.*) A duel, papa ?

Door. Very well. Yes, my child. I didn't wish you to know—it escaped from me. Your father is going to fight.

Mrs. D. With whom ?

Door. With a colonel of the Louisiana Tigers.

Mrs. D. *and* Jos. (*Frightened.*) Oh, good heavens !

Door. To-morrow, in the woods, at the corner of Strawberry Mansion.

Mrs. D. (*Going to him.*) But you are a fool—you, a husband and a father.

Door. Mrs. Dooner, I despise duelling, but there are circumstances when a man owes it to his honor. (*Aside, looking at letter.*) Where is Alice ?

Mrs. D. No—impossible. I will not permit it. (*She goes to table and writes.*) To the Chief of the Police.

[*Enter* ALICE.]

Al. Dinner is served.

[*Enter* Mrs. SPOOPENDYKE *and* CLARA. *Business.*]

Door. (*Approaching* ALICE, *and low.*) This letter to its address : it's very important. (*Retires.*)

Hor. (*Low to* ALICE.) This letter to its address immediately : it's very important. (*He retires.*)

Mrs. D. (*Low to Alice.*) This letter immediately : it's very important.

Jos. (*Aside.*) I will tell Mr. Willie. Come, ladies, dinner.

[*Exit* 3.

Mrs. D. (*Before exit, to* ALICE.) Chut !

Hor. (*Same.*) Chut !

Door. (*Same.*) Chut ! [*They exit together*.

Al. (*Alone, reading.*) To the Chief of Police. I shall only have one trip.

CURTAIN.

ACT IV.

NE.—*An ornate villa garden. Handsome villa with piazzas or balconies and mansard, at the left of stage. Practicable door to villa. Shrubbery, foliage, flowers, etc., along the right of stage. Garden furniture, vases, statuary, etc., grouped about. Ornamental garden wall across back of stage, with door or gate, practicable, in wall c. Beyond this, a row of trees or cut-wood, very open ; back of which are set-houses, or modern street-wings, backed by foliage, garden, or wood—the whole giving the appearance of a shaded street back of the wall, with villas on the opposite side of the street.*

[HORACE *entering at back from the left.*]

HOR. Ten o'clock ; the appointment is not before twelve. (*He approaches pavilion and makes a sign.*) S-s-t ! Mr. Dooner.

DOON. (*Sticking head out.*) Ah, it's you. Don't make a noise —in a minute I am with you. (*He re-enters.*)

HOR. (*Alone.*) Poor Mr. Dooner. He must have passed a miserable night. Luckily the duel will not take place.

DOON. (*Coming out with mantle, military air, belt with two pairs of large pistols underneath.*) Behold me : I am ready !

HOR. How do you find yourself ?

DOON. Calm, like bronze.

HOR. I have some pistols in the carriage.

DOON. (*Showing them.*) I have some also.

HOR. Two pairs.

DOON. One might miss fire. I don't want to be embarrassed by such an accident.

HOR. (*Aside.*) By Jove, he's got it in him. (*Aloud.*) The carriage is at the door when you wish.

DOON. A moment. What time is it ?

HOR. Ten o'clock.

DOON. I don't want to arrive before noon, nor after. (*Aside.*) That might spoil all.

HOR. You are right. (*Aside.*) That might spoil all.

DOON. I am waiting for Hucklestone. I wrote him last night.

HOR. Ah, here he is !

[HUCKLESTONE *entering gate* c.]

HUCK. I received your letter. . I demanded leave of absence. What is it about ?

DOON. Hucklestone, I go to fight in two hours.

HUCK. You ! Nonsense ; and with what ?

DOON. (*Opening mantle.*) With these.

HUCK. Pistols !

DOON. And I count upon you to be my second. (HORACE *goes up.*)

HUCK. Upon me ? Permit me, my friend : that's impossible.

DOON. Why ?

HUCK. It's necessary for me to go to the sugar refinery. I shall be discharged.

DOON. But you have obtained leave of absence.

HUCK. Not to be a second. The law deals with seconds.

DOON. It appears to me, Mr. Hucklestone, that I have rendered you enough services—that you ought not to refuse to assist me in a case where my life may be endangered.

HUCK. (*Aside.*) That's his miserable $300.

DOON. But if you fear to compromise yourself. If you are afraid—

HUCK. I am not afraid. First, I am not free. You think I am chained by the ties of gratitude. Ah, gratitude !

HOR. (*Aside.*) Another !

HUCK. I ask of you only one thing. That is to return by two o'clock. I will pay you immediately, and then we are quits.

HOR. (*Comes down L.*) It's time to start. (*To* DOONER.) If you desire to say good-by to Mrs. Dooner and your daughter—

DOON. No ; I wish to avoid a scene. There would be tears and lamentations. They would throw their arms around me and clutch my cloak to detain me. Let us go. (*Singing off.*) My daughter.

[*Enter* JOSEPHINE, *singing.*]

JOS. Tra la-la-la—(*Speaking.*) Ah, it's you, my good little papa.

DOON. Yes—you see—I leave with these two gentlemen. It is necessary. (*Embrace with emotion.*) Farewell.

JOS. (*Tranquil.*) Good-by, papa. (*Aside.*) There's nothing to fear. Mamma has informed the police, and I have informed Mr. Willie. (*She goes to arrange her flowers.*)

DOON. (*Wiping his eyes.*) Never mind ; don't weep. If you never see me again—think sometimes— (*Stopping.*) Why, she is fixing her bouquet.

HUCK. It's revolting.

[*Enter* MRS. DOONER *with some flowers in her hand.*]

MRS. D. (*To* DOONER.) My love, can I cut a few dahlias ?

DOON. My wife !

MRS. D. I am culling a bouquet for my vase.

DOON. Cull, at such a moment ! I can refuse you nothing. I am about to leave, Caroline.

MRS. D. Oh, you are going out then ?

DOON. Yes I go—out—there, with these two gentlemen.

MRS. D. Go along. Don't be late for dinner.

DOON. (*Aside.*) Hai! This tranquillity! Does my wife no longer love me?

HUCK. All the Dooners are heartless, that's sure.

HOR. It's time, if you wish to be at the rendezvous by twelve.

DON. (*Lively.*) Precise!

MRS. D. (*Lively.*) You have no time to lose.

JOS. Hurry, papa.

DOON. Yes, we go. Caroline, my daughter, farewell! (*He goes up.*)

[*Enter* WILLIE.]

WILL. Stay, Mr. Dooner. The duel will not take place.

ALL. How?

JOS. (*Aside.*) I was sure Willie would arrange it.

MRS. D. But explain to us.

WILL. It's very simple. I have just put Colonel Baumgartner in Moyamensing.

ALL. Moyamensing!

HOR. My rival is very active.

WILL. Yes, that was arranged over a month since between the Colonel and myself, and I couldn't find a better occasion to make myself agreeable to him (*to* DOONER), and to relieve you.

MRS. D. Ah, sir, what a friend!

JOS. (*Low.*) You are our savior.

DOON. (*Aside.*) Ah, that doesn't suit me. I had arranged my little affair so well. At a quarter before twelve a policeman would step between us.

MRS. D. (*To* DOONER.) Thank him.

DOON. Who?

MRS. D. Mr. Rittenhouse.

DOON. (*To* WILLIE, *dryly.*) Ah, yes, sir, I thank you.

HUCK. (*Aside.*) You'd think it would strangle him. (*Aloud.*) I go to touch my salary. (*To* HORACE.) Do you believe the cashier has commenced to pay?

HOR. Yes, without doubt. I have a carriage. I will convey you. Mr. Dooner, we will see each other. You have an answer to give me.

MRS. D. (*Low to* WILLIE.) Stay. Dooner has promised to decide to-day; the moment is favorable.

WILL. Do you believe that he will?

JOS. (*Low.*) Courage, Mr. Rittenhouse.

WILL. You! Oh what happiness!

HUCK. Good-by, Dooner.

HOR. Madam, Miss Josephine. (*Bowing.*)

[*Exit* JOSEPHINE *and* MRS. DOONER R., HUCKLESTONE *and* HORACE *by the back* L.

DOON. (*Who in the mean time has taken off his mantle, pistols, and belt. Aside.*) I am very much annoyed, very much annoyed.

I passed part of the night in writing to my friends that I was going to fight. I shall appear ridiculous.

WILL. (*Aside.*) He ought to be well disposed. We will try. (*Aloud.*) My dear Mr. Dooner?

DOON. (*Dryly.*) Sir!

WILL. I was more fortunate than I expected—to be able to terminate this little affair.

DOON. (*Aside.*) Always his little air of protector. (*Aloud.*) As for me, sir, I regret that you have deprived me of the pleasure of giving a lesson to this professor of spelling.

WILL. How? Then you don't know your adversary is—

DOON. Is an ex-Colonel of the Louisiana Tigers. Very well, what then? I esteem the Tigers, but I am one of those men who know how to look them in the face. (*He passes proudly before.*)

AL. (*Announcing.*) Colonel Bumgartner!

DOON. Hai!

WILL. He?

DOON. You told me that he was in prison.

COL. (*Entering.*) I was there, but I am out. Ah, Mr. Rittenhouse, I shall arrange to take up that check immediately.

WILL. All right, Colonel. I presume you excuse my action. You appeared to be so desirous to be put in prison.

COL. Oh, I like to be in Moyamensing. But not those days that I have arranged to fight. (*To* DOONER.) I am pained, sir, to have made you wait. I am at your orders.

DOON. I think, sir, that you will do me the justice to believe that I was an entire stranger to the action taken by my—

WILL. Entirely, entirely. At this very instant the gentleman expressed his regrets at not being able to meet you.

COL. (*To* DOONER.) I never doubted, sir, that you would be a loyal adversary.

DOON. (*With hauteur.*) I am pleased to hope so, sir.

AL. Dooner is game.

COL. My second and surgeon are at the door. Let us leave.

DOON. Leave?

COL. (*With watch.*) It is twelve o'clock.

DOON. (*Aside.*) Twelve already—then it's past a quarter before.

COL. We will be there in an hour and a half.

DOON. (*Aside.*) An hour and a half. There won't be a policeman within a mile.

WILL. What will you do?

DOON. I—I—have, gentlemen! I have always thought that there was something noble in a man's acknowledging his errors.

COL. *and* ALICE. Hai!

WILL. What did he say?

DOON. Alice, leave us.

WILL. I will retire also.

COL. Oh pardon me. I desire all that passes should be before a witness.

WILL. But—

COL. I beg you to remain.

DOON. Colonel, you are one of those brave soldiers who— And I—I admire those brave soldiers who—I recall that I have in a measure —and I beg you to believe that—(*Aside.*) Hang it ! before my servant. (*Aloud.*) I beg you to believe that it was not my intention—(*Makes sign for* ALICE *to go out, who pretends not to see it.*) (*Aside.*) I'll discharge her to-night. (*Aloud.*) No intention in my thought. No thought—thought—in my intention—to offend a man whom I esteem, and whom I honor.

AL. (*Aside.*) He wilts !

COL. Then, sir, this is an apology.

WILL. (*Quick.*) Oh—his regrets.

DOON. Don't interrupt. Don't interrupt. Let the Colonel speak.

COL. Are they regrets or apologies ?

DOON. A little of one and a little of the other.

COL. Sir, you have written plainly on a certain hotel register, " The Colonel is a—"

DOON. I retire the expression. I take it back.

COL. You take it back here. But there, at Niagara, it is written where all travellers can read it.

DOON. Oh, my heavens ! As for that, you wouldn't expect me to go there to efface it.

COL. I should not have dared ask as much ; but since you offer to do it—-

DOON. I !

COL. I accept.

DOON. Permit me.

COL. Oh I don't demand that you shall depart to-day. No, but to-morrow.

DOON *and* WILL. How ?

COL. How ? By the first train. And you will scrape out yourself gracefully—the two ugly lines that escaped from your pen. That will oblige me.

DOON. Yes. So it seems I must return to Niagara.

COL. The hotel is in Clifton ; we are in Philadelphia.

DOON. Philadelphia ! City of Brotherly Love.

AL. Not a bit of it.

COL. (*Ironically.*) There remains for me nothing but to render homage to your sentiments of conciliation.

DOON. I don't like to shed blood.

COL. (*Smiling.*) I declare myself completely satisfied. (*To* WILLIE.) Mr. Rittenhouse, I have some more checks in circulation. If any should pass through your hands, I will arrange them immediately. Gentlemen, I have the honor to salute you—

DOON. (*Bowing*) Colonel. [*Exit* COLONEL.

AL. (*Sorrowfully.*) That settles that.

Doon. (*Scolding.*) You—I'll settle you. Pack your trunk, blockhead !

AL. (*Stupefied.*) Ah ! What have I done ? [*Exit.*

Doon. (*Aside.*) There is nothing to say. I have apologized. I, of whom they are going to make a picture at the Academy. But whose fault ? This Mr. Rittenhouse's.

WILL. (*Aside.*) Poor man. I don't know what to say to him.

Doon. (*Aside.*) Isn't he going ? He has perhaps some more services to render me.

WILL. Mr. Dooner ?

Doon. Sir.

WILL. Yesterday when I left here I went to my friend the Custom House officer. I spoke to him about your affair.

Doon. You are too good.

WILL. It's arranged. The complaint is withdrawn.

Doon. Indeed !

WILL. Only you write the officer a few words of regret.

Doon. That's it—more apologies, more excuses. Why do you meddle with it ?

WILL. But—

Doon. Is it impossible for you to avoid meddling with my affairs ?

WILL. How—

Doon. Oh, you touch everything ! Who asked you to have the Colonel arrested ? But for you we should have been on the ground at twelve o'clock.

WILL. But nothing prevented your going at two.

Doon. It isn't the same thing.

WILL. Why ?

Doon. Why ? Because—no—you shall not know why. Enough of services, sir. Enough. If I fall into the rapids I beg you to let me go over. I prefer to give the driver $20. There is nothing to be proud of. That's what it costs—$20. I beg of you also not to change the hours of my duels.

WILL. But, Mr. Dooner—

Doon. I don't like people who take things on themselves. It shows indiscretion.

WILL. Permit me.

Doon. No, sir. Nobody lords it over me. Not Dooner. Enough, sir, enough. [*Exit by pavilion.*

WILL. (*Alone.*) I can't understand it. I'm absolutely amazed.

[*Enter* JOSEPHINE]

Jos. Ah, Mr. Willie !

WILL. Miss Josephine !

Jos. Have you interviewed papa ?

WILL. Yes, miss.

Jos. Very well.

Will. I desire to learn the reason for his wonderful antipathy.

Jos. Antipathy! Impossible!

Will. He has just reproached me for pulling him out of the rapids. I believe he was going to offer me $20 as a recompense.

Jos. Absurd!

Will. He told me that was the price.

Jos. But, it's horrible, such ingratitude.

Will. I find that my presence annoys him, and there remains nothing, miss, but to take my leave.

Jos. Not at all. Remain.

Will. For what good? He reserves your hand for Horace!

Jos. Mr. Wallbridge. But I don't wish it.

Will. Ah!

Jos. (*Remembering.*) My mother doesn't wish it. She doesn't partake of papa's sentiment. She has some gratitude—mamma. She likes you. A little while since, she said to me, Mr. Willie is an honest gentleman, a man of heart, and that which I hold dearest in the world I would give to him.

Will. But that which she holds dearest—is you.

Jos. (*Naive.*) I believe so.

Will. Oh, miss! how much I thank you!

Jos. But it's mamma whom you must thank.

Will. And you, miss. Permit me to hope that you will have the same consideration.

Jos. (*Embarrassed.*) Me, sir?

Will. Oh, speak, I pray!

Jos. (*Drooping eyes.*) Sir, when a young lady has been well brought up, she thinks always just like her mother. (*She flies out.*)

Will. (*Alone.*) She loves me. She has said it. Oh, I am oo happy!

[*Enter* Horace.]

Hor. Good-day, Will.

Will. It's you! (*Aside.*) Poor boy!

Hor. Now is the time for philosophy. Mr. Dooner will return. In ten minutes we will have our answer. My poor friend!

Will. Why so?

Hor. In the campaign in which we have been engaged, you have committed fault upon fault.

Will. I!

Hor. Hold! I like you, Will, and I will give you some good advice, that will serve you another time. You have one mortal fault.

Will. Which one?

Hor. You like too well to be of service. It's an unhappy passion with you.

WILL. (*Laughing.*) Ah, indeed !

HOR. Believe me, I am a little older and have observed more of the world than you. Before obliging a man, make yourself sure first that the man is not an idiot.

WILL. Why ?

HOR. Because an idiot is incapable of long supporting that burden to the soul which is called gratitude. They have a constitution so delicate.

WILL. Go on ; develop your riddle.

HOR. Do you wish an example ? Mr. Dooner.

DOON. (*Sticking out head.*) My name.

HOR. You will permit me to express an opinion that he is not a very superior man. (DOONER *disappears.*) Very well. Mr. Dooner has turned against you.

WILL. I am afraid he has.

HOR. After saving his life, you believed, perhaps, that he would remember with pleasure your act of devotion. No, he remembers only three things—First, that he doesn't know how to swim ; second, that he did wrong in going so near the bank ; third, that he made a ridiculous figure with his wet clothes.

WILL. Very well ; but—

HOR. And as it was necessary for him to make a display of fireworks, you have demonstrated to him, as plainly as two and two make four, that you do not believe in his courage by preventing his duel, which would not have taken place.

WILL. Why ?

HOR. I had taken my measures. I do a generous action.

WILL. Certainly you do.

HOR. But I cover my tracks. I hide when I penetrate the weaknesses of my fellow-creatures. It is like going into a powder magazine. I never carry a light.

WILL. So you conclude that it is best never to oblige any one ?

HOR. Oh, no ! But it's necessary to know the mental calibre of the men you oblige. I presume Dooner detests you ; your presence humiliates him.

WILL. But that is ingratitude.

HOR. Ingratitude is a variety of the animal. One amiable philospher has said that ingratitude is the independence of the heart. Therefore, Mr. Dooner is a pork-packer, the most independent of all pork-packers in the country. I discovered it immediately ; so I followed a course exactly opposite to yours.

WILL. How ?

HOR. I let myself down on to a large ledge of rock—as safe as this ground.

WILL. On purpose ?

HOR. Don't you understand ? Give a pork-packer the chance to save a fellow-creature without danger to himself, and it's a master stroke. Since that day I am his joy, his triumph, the symbol of his bravery. As soon as I appear his face glows, his stomach expands. He spreads all his peacock feathers. I hold him as vanity holds the man. When he cools I reanimate him. I exploit him in the newspapers at twenty cents a line.

WILL. Ah, bah ! It was you.

HOR. By Heavens ! To morrow I commence to have him painted in oil, *tête-à-téte* with the Falls. I asked of the artist a very small Niagar*a* and an immense Dooner. In fine, my dear Willie, remember this well—such men do not attach themselves to us by reason of the service we render them, but by reason of the service they render us.

WILL. The men, it's possible ; but the women ?

HOR. Very well, the women.

WILL. They comprehend gratitude ; they know how to guard in the bottom of their heart of hearts the remembrance of a generous action.

HOR. Heavens ! what a pretty speech !

WILL. Luckily Mrs. Dooner does not partake of the sentiments of her husband.

HOR. The mamma is perhaps for you ; but I have for me the superb vanity of the father. My ledge of rocks under Niagara protects me.

[DOONER, *with* MRS. DOONER, JOSEPH, MRS. SPOOPENDYKE, *and* CLARA, *enter from house. He is very grave.*]

DOON. Gentlemen, I am happy to find you together. You have each done me the honor to ask for the hand of my daughter. You shall now hear my decision.

WILL. (*Aside.*) The moment has arrived.

DOON. (*Smiling.*) Mr. Horace, my friend.

WILL. (*Aside.*) I am lost.

DOON. I have already done much for you. I wish to do something more yet—I wish to give you- -

HOR. (*Thanking.*) Ah, sir !

DOON. (*Coldly.*) A little advice. (*Low.*) Don't speak so loud, when you are near a window.

HOR. (*Astonished.*) Nonsense !

DOON. Yes, I thank you for the lesson. (*Aloud.*) Mr. Willie, you have not obtained the footing of your friend. You calculated less, but you please me more. I give you my daughter.

WILL. Ah, sir !

DOON. And observe, I do not think to acquit myself of what I owe to you. I shall always rest under the greatest obligations. Because (*looking at* HORACE) none but idiots are incapable of long supporting that burthen to the soul which is called gratitude. (*He goes near the* R. MR. DOONER *passes* JOSEPHINE *to the side of* WILLIE, *who gives her his arm.*)

HOR. (*Aside.*) Trapped !

WILL. (*Aside.*) Poor Horace !

HOR. I am beaten. (*To* WILLIE.) After as before. Come, give me the hand.

WILL. With all my heart.

HOR. (*Going to* DOONER.) Ah, Mr. Dooner, you listen at doors.

DOON. O my heavens! A father ought to search, to inquire, to listen. (*Taking him aside.*) See here, now truly, did you fall off the step on purpose?

HOR. Where—there?

DOON. On the ledge of rocks under the Falls.

HOR. Yes, but I won't tell a soul.

DOON. Don't. (*Hands. Places.*)

MRS. S. Mr. Dooner?

DOON. The Baby Mine.

MRS. S. Which is the one?

DOON. Ah, yes! (*Calling.*) Mr. Walbridge?

HOR. Mr. Dooner.

DOON. May I request your arm for Miss Clara?

HOR. With pleasure. May I? (*Offering arm to* CLARA.)

CLA. My, it's so absurd!

[*Enter* HUCKLESTONE.]

HUCK. Mr. Dooner, I got my salary at ten o'clock, and I kept the carriage of this gentleman to bring you as soon as possible the three hundred dollars. Here it is.

DOON. But that didn't press.

HUCK. Pardon me, it did press. And now we are quits. Completely quits.

DOON. When I think I was like that—

HUCK. (*To* HORACE.) Here is the number of your carriage. (*Giving card.*) An hour and three quarters.

DOON. Mr. Willie, we shall be at home to-morrow evening, and if you will do us the pleasure to come and take a cup of tea—

COL. BAUMGARTNER. (*Entering.*) Beg pardon, ladies, gentlemen! (*Bowing.*) Mr. Dooner, I left a memorandum. Ah, this must be it! (*Picks up paper and appears to read.*)

WILL. (*Crosses to* DOONER. *Low.*) To-morrow. Do you not think? your promise to the Colonel?

DOON. Ah, that is just. (*Aloud.*) My wife, my daughter, we leave to-morrow for Niagara.

ALL. (*Astonished.*) Hai! What?

MRS. D. Ah, indeed! We have but just arrived. Why return?

DOON. Why? How can you ask? Do you not guess, my dear wife, that I wish to revisit the place where Willie saved my life?

MRS. D. But, Cadwallader!

DOON. Enough, Caroline, the trip is commanded (*glancing back at the Colonel*)—commanded by gratitude!

CURTAIN.

www.ingramcontent.com/pod-product-compliance
Lightning Source LLC
Chambersburg PA
CBHW030904260626
47169CB00008B/2679